Captured by the Cyborg

By

Cara Bristol

Captured by the Cyborg

Copyright © March 2016 by Cara Bristol

ISBN-10: 0-9961452-7-3

ISBN-13 978-0-9961452-7-5

Editor: Kate Richards

Copy Editor: Nanette Sipe

Cover Artist: Sweet 'N Spicy Designs

Formatting by Wizards in Publishing

Published in the United States of America

Cara Bristol

http://www.carabristol.com

This e-book is a work of fiction. While reference might be made to actual historical events or existing locations, the names, characters, places and incidents are either the product of the author's imagination or are used fictitiously, and any resemblance to actual persons, living or dead, business establishments, events, or locales is entirely coincidental.

Captured by the Cyborg

Sometimes the biggest risk is to one's heart....

An ex-Cyber Operations field agent, Dale Homme has kissed danger and betrayal more times than he cares to count. Now he runs a clandestine factory beneath the surface of the moon Deceptio, where confidentiality and security matter more than anything. When a beautiful young woman arrives seeking a job, Dale knows within minutes she's lying. Everything about her is false: her past, the people she claims to know, her reason for being on Deceptio. Illumina Smith? Even her name is an alias. Logic says send her packing. His gut says she's in trouble. She needs him. So he'll do anything to keep her safe...even if it means keeping her captive.

Chapter One

"What's wrong, Baby? Why can't you fly?" Dale rubbed his neck as he pored over test data for the ZX7M, a high-speed luxury spacecraft nicknamed Baby because she'd proven as temperamental and unpredictable as a colicky infant.

After performing flawlessly in computer simulations, Baby stalled out in test flights. The Xenian emperor who'd ordered her had begun pushing for delivery, his patience nearing an end. If they didn't hand her over soon—or if she failed to perform as promised, Moonbeam Chop Shop could kiss good-bye the option for any future contracts.

Baby hadn't been built to be a single, unique spacecraft, but to be the prototype for an entire fleet. A contract of that magnitude would provide financial security for years.

For his 152 employees.

For himself, Dale didn't need security of any kind. Too much security bred complacency and boredom.

Boredom led to dissatisfaction. He puffed out his

cheeks and expelled a long breath. *This was what you wanted. You chose this.* Most people would consider his business, which sometimes operated on the shady side of galactic law, exciting—but it didn't deliver the adrenalin rush he'd gotten from being a field operative. He didn't think he'd miss Cyber Operations when he left, but he did.

Ping! The microprocessor embedded in his brain signaled an incoming communication.

Hey, boss. I'm on site and settled in. The message stream shooting into Dale's head originated from Charlie's computer.

Welcome back! Dale greeted his assistant. How was R&R?

Stellar—until I got some bad news before I boarded the shuttle.

Oh?

Meemaw isn't doing well. Mom says she might not last much longer.

I'm sorry to hear that. You sure you're ready to come back to work? Maybe you'd rather be with her? His assistant often talked about his grandmother, and on his desk kept a stillvid of a vital steel-haired lady with eyes to match who looked like she kicked some serious ass. The possibility of losing her must be very hard on him.

Thanks, I appreciate that, but there's nothing I can do. I'll check on her during my next leave. I don't want to dwell on what might happen, so I'm happy to be back on Deceptio and working again.

What else would one say to the boss? If the comment had come from anyone else, he would have assumed the guy was blowing smoke up his ass, but Charlie's enthusiasm for his job had always seemed genuine.

Well, I'm glad to have you back, he said, even though he didn't begrudge any employee furlough. A person could only spend so much time underground before he went nuts—which was why Moonbeam had a brig in addition to a generous leave policy. Just in case. So far, R&R had done the trick, and no one had snapped.

Maybe that was the source of his dissatisfaction—he didn't follow his own policy. He'd been off moon for business, but how long had it been since he'd taken a vacation? One year, four months, and twelve days, his microprocessor reported. Too long.

Being stuck on Deceptio also eliminated the chance for feminine companionship. He was the boss. Nothing good could come of getting involved with an employee so he lived by a strict hands-off personal code, which he'd never violated.

How long had it been since he'd gotten laid?

One—his cyberbrain started to tell him, but he cut off the information. That kind of data he didn't need to know.

Andrew do okay? Charlie asked.

He did fine, but he's not you. The fill-in had been capable—all Moonbeam employees were competent or they wouldn't be here, but, as owner, Dale dealt with confidential proprietary matters and needed an assistant he could trust without reservation. No substitute could fill Charlie's shoes.

That's what I like to hear. Job security. Speaking of jobs, the candidates for the Diagnostics and Repair position have arrived. They're scheduled to meet with March, and the ones who pass his muster will be sent to you.

Great. When Moonbeam's computer experts hadn't been able to figure out Baby's problem, Dale had sought outside help. Headhunters had combed the galaxy for months to recruit candidates with the right skill set *and* the willingness to tolerate Deceptio's working and living conditions. Time had about run out. Whether a newbie could get up to speed on Baby's systems and then figure out the problem before the craft had to be delivered was doubtful. At this point, he was desperate, out of options. *How many candidates are there?*

Six. Originally eight, but three decided before they boarded the shuttle they didn't want the job, and then there was a last minute add-on.

Par for the course. Not only were workers sworn to secrecy, unable to share the details of their jobs, but the Moonbeam remanufacturing plant was located a kilometer below the barren surface of Deceptio. Staff lived and worked underground for months at a time—until scheduled R&R allowed them to venture off moon.

Nor were employees told where in the galaxy they were. Transport to and from Deceptio occurred in blackout. Only a select handful of managers and carefully vetted test pilots knew the coordinates. Even Charlie didn't know.

Dale pushed back from his chair and strode to the glass wall overlooking the factory floor. His cyber-enhanced vision zoomed in on the job candidates sitting in a row across from Charlie's desk. Four men, one woman...and a *child*?

A kid is interviewing?

Charlie glanced up at the window. His assistant, who had normal 20/20 human vision, couldn't see him from the distance, even if the glass wasn't a two-way mirror. *You mean the blonde girl?*

Yeah. Is she a prodigy?

No, just a petite adult female. She's the last-minute addition, so you haven't seen her application.

If she hadn't perched on the edge of the seat, her feet wouldn't have touched the floor. The other candidates chatted among themselves, no doubt comparing impressions of their experiences so far, but she sat disengaged from the others, her chair a discreet distance away, her hands folded in her lap.

Curious.

Why don't you send her up?

Now?

Yes.

Hold on; let me shoot you her CV.

A split second later her curriculum vitae popped up. *Illumina Smith. Female. Age 24.* Graduated with honors from the Terran Cyberscience Institute. Four years as a programmer with Infinity AI Corporation. Given her youth, she didn't have longevity behind her, but the qualifications she did have were impressive. TCI was recognized throughout the galaxy for its excellence. Its graduates were highly sought after. And, Infinity, the number one android manufacturer, hired the best of the best. Job seekers would kill to work for them. So why leave? A good question for the interview.

I'm ready. Send her up.

Charlie motioned to the woman and then pointed to the stairs leading to Dale's office. He turned away from the window and removed computer debris from a chair. Moments later, a brisk tap sounded outside. He opened the door.

Petite adult? Try sprite. The woman's head didn't reach his shoulder. But what she lacked in stature, she compensated for with hair.

Shimmering, silvery-blonde waves of it tumbled to her hips. The platinum shade didn't reflect light, it *radiated* it, almost as if the individual strands were composed of fibers of light itself. Although women could and did take chemical supplements to alter pigment at the cellular level, and platinum hair was not unusual, the combined effect of the color and shine was. Striking under the harsh artificial illumination—what would it look like in moonlight?

In a complete violation of propriety, he reached

out to touch. He caught himself and snapped his hand to his side, calling upon his nanocytes to stamp out the kindling of desire. Turned on by a job candidate's hair. This is what happened when you didn't get laid often enough. Not entirely his fault though. He'd planned to visit the Darius 4 pleasure resort, until Lamis-Odg terrorists had destroyed the place. Under reconstruction, reopening hadn't been scheduled yet.

He forced his attention away from her hair.

And noticed her clothing. What the *hell* was she wearing? Masculine, almost military-style trousers in a fabric mottled in various shades of tan led to clunky coyote-brown boots. A loose-fitting jacket in the same variegated pattern covered her top half. Fatigues— but from what century? The twenty-first maybe? Where had she acquired the getup?

"Mr. Homme?" Gray eyes met his in a direct stare. "I'm Illumina Smith. Thank you for seeing me." Her voice tinkled like chimes blowing in a gentle wind, but the hand that seized his gripped like a steel clamp.

It's not an arm wrestling match. He hid his amusement while noting the slenderness of her bone structure. His thumb and index finger would overlap

8

if he were to encircle her wrist. "Come in. Have a seat." He gestured.

She lurched with a jerky, awkward gait to the chair and sat, her posture rigid. Her robotic movement was so opposite the grace he'd expected, he ran a quick scan. No, not android. An organic, sentient life-form, but not human either.

"Your name is very unusual." He plopped into his sensa-chair, which immediately conformed to the shape of his body and began a massage.

A tiny furrow creased her forehead. "Smith is a common Terran surname."

If she was Terran, he was a six-eyed, webbed-handed Arcanian. "I meant Illumina."

"Oh," she said, and for a split second her skin turned luminescent.

A normal human wouldn't have noticed the brief flash, but a cyborg with enhanced vision caught it right away. "How was the flight?" he asked. To protect the location of the installation, interviewees had been picked up at a central planet and transported via a windowless spacecraft.

"Smooth. The stewards were very attentive."

"Good to know," he said. "I'm curious, how did you hear about this position?"

"Cy-Net. I saw a posting." She paused. "Although it didn't give a lot of information. It was rather cryptic."

"And that encouraged you to apply?"

"Actually, yes."

Ads were worded to be vague, but coded with keywords to attract individuals with the right skill set. In his mind's eye, he scanned through the documents Charlie had transmitted with her CV to verify she'd signed the confidentiality statement. She had.

"So, what do you know of what we do here?" he asked.

"I understand you need a computer troubleshooter; I got that much from the ad. After arriving and seeing the vehicles, I surmise you need a programmer to work on spacecraft."

"And are you that person?"

She didn't blink. "I am. You could say I have a way with coding."

"Why did you leave Infinity? They're one of the top artificial intelligence companies."

"They're an excellent company, but I've always been interested in things that fly. To work on shuttles and other spacecraft would be a dream come true."

Luminescence flashed again.

Interesting. Dale steepled his fingers. "You didn't know what the job involved until you got here."

"There...were hints, bolstered by comments the recruiter made when he offered me the interview." She lifted her chin. "What I'm not sure is why everything is so hush-hush."

Fair enough. "Moonbeam Chop Shop disassembles and remanufactures spacecraft. We can transform a pleasure cruiser into a fighter. When vehicles leave here, they're unregistered to any planetary agency, which is the way our clients like it. Further, we've developed cloaking technology that can render a spacecraft invisible to the eye and computer scans. We want to protect our proprietary information." And since not everything Moonbeam did was technically on the up-and-up, it was best to run a clandestine operation. For that reason, the runway was cloaked, too.

"I understand," she said.

"I'm looking for a programmer to troubleshoot anomalies. The vehicles we acquire often come installed with alien electronics. Our knowledge base increases the more ships we work on, but we continue to encounter challenges." Like Baby. What the hell was causing the malfunction? She wasn't even a remanufactured craft. They'd designed and built her from the ground up. "Often there are glitches in programming or code hidden within code that can be difficult to detect, override, or remove."

"Troubleshooting is my specialty. If I can get my hands on a system, I can figure it out," she boasted, but Dale sensed her self-confidence was genuine. Whether she could do what she claimed remained to be seen, but *she* believed it.

"Do you understand how isolated you'll be if I hire you for this position? You won't be able to leave the facility until your furlough. You'll work here—and live in the employee barracks. For months at a time, you won't see sunlight, hear a bird chirp or an insect sing, or feel the wind on your face. You'll be stuck with the same people day in and day out—and, by the way, there will be no natural rotation to mark the time. Day and night are controlled by artificial lighting and work schedules. The only visitors to Deceptio are pre-approved buyers or sellers. For security reasons, you won't be permitted contact with any outsiders, including your family."

Her lips twitched with a slight smile. "You make it sound so appealing."

"Many people can't handle the isolation. We lose a lot of good employees to moon fever." He opened up a hailing frequency in his cyberbrain and fired off a couple of messages.

"That won't happen with me, Mr. Homme."

"They all say that," he said.

She leaned forward. "I mean it."

Why would a young woman leave a prestigious, lucrative job to live in an artificial environment beneath the surface of a barren moon? Moonbeam paid as much if not more than Infinity, and offered generous leave, but that was the extent of the perks. For a programmer starting out in her career, Infinity was the better choice. Which led him to believe she was running *from* something, rather than *to* something. "Tell me about your educational background."

She eased back, but her spine didn't touch the frame of the chair. "I graduated with honors from TCI."

"I got that from your CV. What was your favorite class?"

"I was on the computer security track, but I also mastered all the computer languages." A response, but not the answer to his question.

Ping! Ping! Both his messages came back with replies. He read them while continuing the interview. Multitasking was a cinch for a cyborg. "You must have taken Professor Annabel Harriot's class. She's a friend of mine."

Illumina nodded, her face flashing that luminescence that caused her to glow like a pearl. "I learned so much from her. She's....tough, but respected."

"So you think you can handle this job?"

"I'm confident I can."

"And the isolation?"

"Won't be a problem."

"If I were to offer you the position, when could you start?"

"Immediately. I, um, brought my suitcase. I don't even need to return home."

Interplanetary hiring laws dictated what an employer could or couldn't ask a prospective job seeker. Dale knew the rules, but he hadn't gotten where he was by following them. Cyberoperatives worked outside the law, as did spacecraft chop shop owners, so he had no qualms about asking whatever he needed to gather the necessary info to facilitate his decision. "What species are you exactly?"

"Ter—" She dropped her gaze to her lap, where her hands locked together. She raised her eyes and bit her lip. "*Faria*," she admitted in a low voice.

It was one of the few truths she'd uttered during the entire interview.

Annabel Harriot did not exist; he had made her up. The professor was as fictitious as the qualifications on Illumina's CV. His contacts at TCI and Infinity had reported they'd never heard of Illumina Smith. To their recollection, she'd never attended the institute or been employed by the AI corporation.

"What happened to your wings?"

She swallowed. "I was…injured, and they were amputated."

That explained her jerky, painful-looking movements, why she'd didn't sit back against the chair. The surgery was probably recent.

"I'm fully recovered. It won't affect my ability to do my job."

"Do you still feel your wings?" he asked, remembering his acute relief upon waking in the hospital to sense his arms and legs, only to discover nothing but air under the bedcovers.

"Yes." A sad smile twisted her mouth. "It only

becomes a problem if I try to fly."

He glanced out the window. The five remaining candidates had strong, *authentic* credentials. Common sense and the security of his installation were in complete agreement: send the wingless, little Faria with the bogus resume packing. Why had she applied for a job for which she was so unqualified?

"Get your stuff. I'll have Charlie, my assistant, show you to the barracks." Instinct overruled logic. "You can start tomorrow."

They'd find something for her to do.

I'm such a sucker.

Chapter Two

"And that's the grand tour." Charlie, Dale Homme's assistant, led the way into a dorm with two beds. "This is your room. You're the only one here now, but when the next female comes on board, you'll have a roomie." He looked at her. "If you'd prefer to have company, I can ask if any of the other women will trade, but being alone will be temporary anyway."

"I don't want to put anyone out. This will be fine." Illumina deposited her bag next to the closest bunk. With any luck, no one would join her anytime soon.

"Well, the women's ChemShower is down the corridor. Breakfast is at 06:00. Orientation starts at seven."

"How long is orientation?"

"There's no set period. It depends on you, what your skills are, how long it takes for you to learn the ropes," Charlie said. Meaning they wouldn't turn her loose until they were confident of her abilities. "Orientation and on-the-job training could take three to four weeks."

People needed a month to get up to speed? She jotted a mental note to dumb down her abilities to avoid arousing suspicion.

"Dinner is served at 19:00 in the mess hall. Do you have any other questions?"

She shook her head. "No, thank you. You've been very helpful." She smiled, at ease with his open, friendly, unthreatening face and manner. So different from Homme, whose shorn hair, fighter body, and hard expression wreaked havoc with her certainty. Ex-military, she'd bet. A rough and tough man's man. Not refined and debonair like Alonio.

Homme had worn his skepticism like a birthday suit. Naked and bold. Laugh lines spraying out from his eyes indicated he wasn't always so serious, but he'd squinted with suspicion throughout the interview.

"If you need anything, you can reach me through any comm module." Charlie pointed to a screen on the wall. "I'd better return to my desk. Welcome to Moonbeam, and congratulations. You must have impressed the hell out of Dale for him to hire you before he'd interviewed anyone else."

He left, and Illumina locked the door behind him

with a palm swipe across the screen. *I did it! I got the job!*

Dizzy, almost buoyant, she could float away. She took a deep breath, filling her lungs with air untainted by fear.

Alonio can't reach me.

The prospect of working and living underground on an out-of-the-way barren lunar satellite might deter some, but the secrecy and isolation sounded like a lifesaver to her.

She shuffled to her bunk and sank onto it. Not as soft as she preferred, but she didn't rest well anyway. Sleeping on her stomach felt odd; lying on her back hurt too much. And then she popped up in a panic at every creak, every structural groan in the middle of the night. Maybe she wouldn't do that here.

I got the job!

Her qualifications read well, but she didn't doubt that others probably had more practical experience than she. How could they not? The only factual data on her CV was her first name and her age. She looked younger than twenty-four, so she hadn't dared to fake more than four years work experience and a degree in computer science she'd never earned.

That didn't mean she wasn't qualified. The fact

that she had hacked into the computer systems of TCI and Infinity and planted her name in their databanks proved she was up to the task of programming a few little spaceships. Her qualification for the position was that she didn't need qualifications.

She was one of the few gifted Faria who were computer sensates. Through touch and telepathy, she could become one with cybersystems and integrate herself into the code. And then slip away without a trace.

Alonio was a sensate, too.

"No matter where you go, I'll find you."

He had. At the medical facility on Faria, she'd barely escaped with her life. The guard outside her room hadn't been so lucky. Alonio had found her again on Harkleon, ThetaTor, and all the other planets, moons, and space stations where she attempted to hide. Two months on the run seemed like years. And, one day, he would catch her.

She'd resigned herself to her doom when she happened upon the help wanted announcement on Cy-Net. *Computer troubleshooter. Secret. Confidential. Nondisclosure agreement required.* The keywords had leaped out like a lifeline. The opportunity had sounded too good to be true, but she would have applied if the job had been cleaning waste recycling tanks.

Communications to and from Moonbeam were encrypted, but that wasn't the reassuring part. Alonio's sensate ability wasn't as developed as hers, but he was still quite clever, and tracking her posed little difficulty. The security of the installation itself gave her hope. *Nothing* had been disclosed about its location. *She* was here and didn't know where here was!

Her ex might figure out who had hired her, but he wouldn't know where to begin to look. If she stayed, *eventually* he would find her—he always did—but by then she would be long gone. When he did manage to root out the general location, he wouldn't be able to get on-site.

"Anyone who assists you will suffer."

Her ex-lifemate would do everything in his considerable power to fulfill his promise. He'd proven it by killing the guard at the infirmity. But if he couldn't get into Deceptio, its employees would be safe.

Not exactly sure what the specific job entailed, she'd hacked into TCI and Infinity and forged a new identity for herself. Illumina Smith. *Terran.* She'd taken a crash course on human culture and language. Her wings were gone, so she only had to hide her natural luminosity and the faint glitter to her skin. Luminosity suppressants helped to conceal the glow she exuded when she lied or got emotional.

She'd affected a tough bravado and adopted military dress to distract attention from her disability: difficulty moving caused by back pain and weak legs. Faria could walk, of course, but they were meant to fly, so their lower limbs were frail. The more she used her legs, the stronger they got, but she tired if she stood or walked for long periods.

She thought she'd pulled off the Terran disguise pretty well, until Homme had pegged her as nonhuman.

What had given her away? If she knew, she'd fix it so she could become one of those employees no one could place. The ones who escaped notice by fading into the background. The less attention she drew, the better. Workers might be bound by confidentiality not to reveal the location or function of Moonbeam, but that didn't mean people didn't gossip. They were prohibited from talking about business, not their co-workers. *Remember that wingless Faria we worked with...*

She was the only wingless Faria in existence.

Was Homme's question about her race legal? Employers weren't supposed to ask about species or origin—not that one couldn't tell from looking. Malodonians had blue skin, Arcanians had webbed fingers and six eyes, Lamis-Odg had ridged foreheads and vestigial horns. Slime crawlers...well, their species name said it all. Faria had wings. Without those specialized appendages, only the tendency to glow would betray her origins. With that under control, there wasn't much to distinguish her from a Terran, hence, her choice of disguise.

When Homme had asked, it had been on the tip of her tongue to lie, but he was already suspicious. To fabricate a falsehood when you would be believed was one thing; to attempt to deceive someone who knew the truth begged for trouble.

If she'd been bolder, she would have thrown the question back at him. "What are *you*?"

Let him wiggle out of that one, because he wasn't the ordinary Terran he tried to pass himself off as. Homme was a cyborg. A computer-enhanced human. A sensate could pick them out a parsec away.

Okay, maybe not that far, but one could tell from a handshake. She'd learned Terrans in business situations greeted each other that way, and that a firm one was preferable to the dead-fish kind. With a strong grip on his hand, she'd sensed his cybernetics.

She'd been tempted to probe his head to search for clues as to what he was looking for in an employee, perhaps to plant a suggestion that she was the right candidate. If he had been an android, lacking self-awareness, she could have slipped in and slid out without him ever realizing he'd been altered. But he was more human than computer, and he would have known in an instant. And, in the end, she hadn't needed the extra edge.

She'd feared he might have caught on to her secrets and lies and rejected her, but then he offered her the job! She could have cried with relief. Kissed him with happiness.

No, never that.

His handshake, which could have crushed her fingers if he'd been so inclined, was all the contact she wanted, thank you very much. Human males were taller than Faria men, and Homme towered at least a half a head over everyone on site. His biceps alone had to be nearly the circumference of her waist. She'd never met a man that large. His office, though generous-sized, had seemed small the way his intimidating bulk and presence took up the space.

Better to keep her distance and avoid him as much as possible. He might ask her more questions. He'd hired her, but that didn't mean she'd escaped all suspicion, and recent events had taught her to maintain her guard. Probably, since Dale Homme owned Moonbeam, he didn't interact with workers on a daily basis anyway. Charlie had already introduced her to March, her future supervisor. As long as she did her job and didn't arouse suspicion, she wouldn't have cause to see Homme very often. He had more important things to do than to concern himself with a lowly troubleshooter. A new hire.

Her stomach rumbled with a hunger she hadn't experienced in a long time. Fear and stress had all but eradicated her appetite. Another reason for the loose-fitting military garb: hide how thin she'd become. She glanced at the monitor on the wall. Four more hours until dinner.

It felt good to be hungry again.

And safe.

Chapter Three

From his office, Dale watched Illumina wheel a cart of diagnostic equipment into a cabinet and then amble awkwardly through the shop toward the mess hall. As if she sensed his scrutiny, she glanced up at the windows. He had the urge to duck out of sight, but he held his ground. *She can't see you.* She turned away and continued on.

Again, her stiff gait struck him as odd, but what caught and held his attention was that incredible hair, the slightness of her frame, the ridiculous attire. Her.

You're a perv, Homme. What was it they used to call men who spied on women? Peeping Toms? The glass wall allowed him to observe the rotation as the vehicles moved from station to station. He couldn't count the number of times in the week since Illumina had come on board that he found himself watching for her.

He needed neither his cybervision nor her distinctive hair to find her amidst the bustling beehive of activity. His human senses were attuned to her, his gaze zooming in like a computer fixing on programmed coordinates.

He had to stop this shit. She was his employee. Messing with the staff violated personal and professional ethics and would be bad for business and morale. *Step away from the window, then.*

He didn't. He waited until she disappeared into the dining room before he returned to his desk. Hiring her had been a mistake. He'd checked further into her background and discovered she'd faked more than credentials; she'd manufactured an entire life. From what he could tell, Illumina Smith did not exist. She'd handed him more than enough grounds for immediate dismissal.

She hadn't lied about her abilities though. After her first day, he'd checked with March, her supervisor, and discovered that she performed exceptionally well, flying through orientation with a natural knack for programming, as if computer code were her native language.

That wasn't why he hadn't fired her yet. He kept her because...

Because although he had a microprocessor embedded in his brain and robotic nanocytes in his blood received and analyzed data in a blink of an eye, human gut instinct told him to hold off on the termination. Honed by his training and experience as a field agent with Cyber Operations, intuition had saved his ass more times than he'd ventured to the window in the past three days.

She was in trouble.

She didn't act like it. He couldn't prove it. But he felt it.

He was a sucker for an underdog. Deceptio's security had to come first, but with that assured, he did what could he could to give people a leg up. Moonbeam was one of the few employers who would hire Arcanians. Having earned a reputation for thievery, Arcanians found it difficult to find honest work. So they resorted to theft. A vicious cycle, which he had tried to break by offering them gainful employment. Arcanians and Faria with secrets weren't the only hard-luck cases he'd hired.

Hey, boss, Baby's coming in, Charlie hailed him.

Dale sat up straight in his chair. *Any word on how she did?*

Haven't heard, but Giorgio was gone longer than usual. I don't know if that's positive or negative.

Dale sighed. Negative would be his guess. The fucking ship had probably stalled out again, and

Giorgio had trouble restarting the engines. Once they'd had to send a tow craft to drag it back in. *Okay, thanks. I'll come down.*

* * * *

The descender, loaded with the spacecraft, came to a stop then rotated. A dolly towed the craft off the lift, and then the docking bridge rolled toward it. Dale gripped the railing as the tool connected and locked into place. The hatch on the ZX7M sprang open, and a small, wiry man in a flight suit crawled out. Giorgio's expression looked grimmer than a Harkleon winter.

Fuck. Again? If he didn't have so much time and money invested, he'd strip the damn ship of its electronics and haul the hull to a recreation station for children to play with. "Well?" He braced for the bad news.

Giorgio's shoulders slumped, and he shook his head. His lips began to twitch, and then his face split into a wide grin. "She flew like a bolt of lightning."

Dale blinked. "You're shitting me."

"Not a single hiccup. She passed the maneuvers at the top of the range. I don't know what magic

30

Diagnostics and Repair pulled out of their hats, but Baby can *fly*. Better and faster than we hoped."

Laughter snorted out Giorgio's nose. "You should have seen your face when you thought it had failed again."

"You're a real comedian." He could find the humor in most things, but his patience had been pushed to the edge by the spacecraft's repeated failures.

"I'll do some more test flights to verify today's results weren't a fluke, but I think the problem is behind us now." Giorgio could be a pain in the ass sometimes—most of the time really—but there was no doubting his dedication to his job.

"That's a good idea. We have to be sure." After four failures, they needed more than one check mark in the success column. Giorgio probably itched to fly Baby when he could enjoy himself and not have to worry about being cast adrift in space.

According to tattletale computer logs, Giorgio occasionally conducted non-test flights and non-regulation maneuvers in violation of company policy. However, he had rocket fuel for blood and was the best pilot Moonbeam had. If the space jockey sneaked off on a lark every now and then, Dale could turn a blind eye to the infraction to keep his most experienced pilot happy.

After they descended the docking scaffold, Giorgio swaggered toward employee mess, and Dale went to hunt down March. The Diagnostics and Repair supervisor sat at his console grinning at a screen full of numbers. "She passed!" March spun around and pumped his fist in the air.

"I heard. Good job!" Dale said. "What was the problem?"

"A shield virus. It changed the computer code, but made it look like the code was correct. "I'll shoot you the test data," he said.

"How did you manage to find it?"

"I didn't. Your new hire did."

"Illumina? Isn't she still in orientation?"

"Not anymore. She breezed through training in a couple of days. We'd discussed the problems with the ZX7M in class, and she asked for a peek at the craft. She came back and reported it fixed. I had my doubts, but she insisted, so Giorgio took the craft for a spin. It's a wonder she found it. Shield viruses are almost impossible to detect."

* * * *

In the employee dining room, Illumina tucked into a platter piled with enough fruits, vegetables, and nut patties to feed two people twice her size. Did she always eat that much or was she compensating? She looked too thin, despite the camouflage of her anachronistic attire. Was that much food typical for a Faria? Maybe flying burned a lot of energy.

Except Illumina didn't fly. She was lucky to be alive. Genetic and biomed info on Faria was scant, but it was common knowledge that removal of their wings resulted in fatal hemorrhage. Against the odds, she'd survived.

He strode toward her. Her eyes widened before she shuttered them behind a neutral expression. "May I join you?" he asked.

"You're the boss." She jutted her chin at a vacant chair.

Dale swung it around and straddled it.

She set down her fork.

"Eat," he said. "Don't let me stop you."

"No, it's all right." She folded her hands in her lap.

"How are you getting along?" He tried not to stare at her plate. How could someone so small consume so much? Of course, she wasn't eating now; he'd interrupted her meal.

"Fine."

"Better than fine, I'd say. I heard you fixed Baby."

"Baby?"

"That's what we call the ZX7M."

"Why?"

"Because she's cranky."

"Oh. That makes sense."

"I wanted to thank you for an extraordinary job." Mostly he wanted an excuse to seek her out.

"You're welcome," she said.

"My cyber team is top-notch, but we might never have discovered the shield virus."

"You have to know what to look for." She ducked her head, but not before a flash of luminescence lit up her cheeks.

"What *did* you look for?" No idle question. If a spacecraft had been infected with a shield virus, it could happen on another. All the techs had to be trained.

She looked up. Her face seemed to glow from within. "The only thing that was left. Your team had eliminated every other possibility."

Simple enough, except his top cyber experts had been stumped for months. Even if her qualifications had been real, they wouldn't add up to the sum of his team's experience.

"How's everything else? The barracks, the food—" he glanced at her plate and then scanned the mess hall. "Have you gotten to know any of the other employees?" Small groups of people were eating together, talking, laughing, but she'd chosen to sit alone.

Already ramrod straight, she stiffened further. "Do you always take such an interest in your workers?"

Friendliness and approachability encouraged crew members to bring problems to his attention. He couldn't fix what he didn't know about, and he much preferred dealing with small issues before they ballooned into crises. He would have commended Illumina for her contribution in any case, but more than positive employee relations had motivated him to seek her out. Truth? He had jumped at the chance to see her.

To touch her, to tangle his hands in her hair, to kiss...

Dale stood up and righted the chair. "I take an

interest in my shop. I won't keep you any longer. Enjoy the rest of your meal." He stalked away. Employees waved and shouted greetings, and he stopped by their tables to chat for a bit. On his way out the door, he halted. He spun on his heel and went back to her table.

He bent his head to her ear and said in a low voice, "If you're running from something, you'd be better served if you tried to blend in by joining the other workers for a meal, instead of sitting alone." He strode out of the mess hall.

* * * *

Alarm ratatatted in her chest with a too-familiar beat. Illumina dragged in air and grabbed for calming thoughts. *Don't panic. Doubt isn't the same as knowledge.*

She'd learned that lesson well. There'd been suspicion about Alonio, but he'd erased the facts, and without concrete knowledge...well, here she was.

She pushed her plate away, appetite replaced by queasiness. Hunger had evaporated the instant she'd sensed the object of her obsession had entered the mess hall. She had a visual eidetic memory, and

36

Dale's image had burrowed into her mind, interrupting an already-fitful sleep with sexual dreams. Disturbing and inappropriate, but at least they crowded out the nightmares.

If she had one wish—beyond guaranteed safety—it would be a night of nothingness, to lay her head on the pillow and drift into the void until morning—or what passed for morning in a sublunar environment.

Way to go.

Only on Deceptio a week, already she'd screwed up the plan to avoid attention. She'd drawn her supervisor's notice by whizzing through his little training program, fixed an "unfixable" spacecraft, and topped it all off by being rude to the big boss and furthering his suspicion.

Illumina studied her co-workers. She hadn't meant to be standoffish, but the idea of engaging in conversation filled her with dread. The other workers would be curious, would ask where she'd come from, where she'd worked in the past—what could she say that wasn't a lie? Every conversation led further into deception. Each lie provided another opportunity to trip up. She'd already proven how easy that was.

But Homme was right. Distance invited gossip, so she would do as he suggested and introduce herself to a tableful of employees and ask to join their group.

Tomorrow.

Tonight she would remain alone and figure out how to eradicate her growing attraction to her boss, who'd stirred out of dormancy a sexual awakening that compelled her to glance at his office dozens of times a day.

Personal contact with her employer would be crazy. Intimacy, disastrous. He wouldn't physically harm her—although she sensed an edge in him—but he threatened her peace of mind, her self-defense plan. He distracted her from the vigilance required for survival. Deceptio was a mere pit stop on a destination-less journey. She would catch her bearings, build up her stamina, and then search for a new place to hide. She'd resigned herself to a life on the run, because it was the only way to elude Alonio. The longer she stayed in one location, the greater the likelihood he would find her, even if there was no record of Moonbeam's existence, and Deceptio was charted as uninhabitable.

Temptation might have convinced her to scratch the itch while she regrouped and attempted to devise a plan, but the microprocessor in Homme's brain made bodily contact fraught with risk. What if, in the heat of passion, she slipped into his mind? Integrated into his software? Altered him as easily as she'd rewritten the code in the ZX7M? It was *unlikely*, but it could happen. Even if she caused no damage, he would feel violated to have her inside his head, privy to the private data stored on his microprocessor. Her personal code of honor would not permit the violation.

She rubbed her temples. Among the rare sensate Faria, she'd been a prodigy, in a class of her own. Her ex, with much more modest abilities, wouldn't have been able to find her so easily except he had an advantage. Their conjugal bond.

He'd been her husband, her *lifemate*.

Only in very few and unique instances did Farian law allow for dissolution. Their case had been one of the exceptions. After the attack, the marriage had been voided, but the law could not dissolve the psychic filaments giving him an edge in finding her. One by one, as she could bring the threads to awareness, she severed them, but she had no idea how many their bonding had forged or how many remained.

"You will always be mine. Till passing do us

part." How loving Alonio's words had sounded—until
she realized the danger bound to the vow. Until his
growing mental instability and bursts of violence had
led her to attempt to annul their union, until he
caught her, until he sliced off her wings and left her
for dead. Until he hunted her to fulfill his promise.

The threat would never cease. He'd proven it.
He'd broken all his vows, except for the one. *Till
passing do us part.*

But for now, at her temporary haven, she could
rest, allow her body to finish healing, and figure out
where to go next. She had to do everything she could
to stay focused on staying alive. Getting involved with
Dale Homme would not further that goal.

Who said anything about getting involved?
Certainly not him. He'd never been anything but
professional. The fire snaking its way through her
veins originated in her alone. Homme had done
nothing deliberate to kindle it, to encourage it, or, in
fact, to indicate any mutuality. Her feeling that he
observed her from his office lair was imagination, a
fruitless fiction she conjured to fill the loneliness,
soothe a longing for connection. Farias mated for life.
Since she'd dissolved her marital union, there would
likely be no other mate for her.

Lust fueled her desire for the cyborg. It stood to reason suppressed physical desires would seek an outlet. *Any space station in a meteor shower.* Except she hadn't noticed a rise in temperature, the tingling and swelling in her feminine core, and the persistence of sexual fantasies until her path had crossed with Dale Homme.

She eyed the males eating in convivial groups. Should she wish to alleviate the problem, the chop shop offered a variety of species from which to choose—many handsome and virile males—and willing, if the glances they shot her way served as an indication. But their interest left her...uninterested.

Not so the one man she'd be wise to avoid. His deep voice and the way it rumbled through her was arousing enough, without the attraction of oddly appealing close-cropped bristly hair, the height and solidity of his muscled body, his confident posture, and how his size dominated the space—so different from Farian slenderness. Never could she have envisioned she'd be attracted to a part-machine, part-human. If anyone would have suggested it, she would have laughed.

Alonio could not match the cyborg's brawn, but he possessed other assets to ensure he won any physical confrontation. She would not endanger her employer by putting him in a position of having to defend her—not that he would. It would not take a losing battle for her to be handed over to her murderous ex-lifemate, only a well-presented argument. She could not meet him without becoming hysterical, and he would argue his side of the "facts" in his calm, convincing way. Dale would believe him the way everyone else had.

She would leave Deceptio long before that happened.

Chapter Four

Dale surveyed his domain. Timers had dimmed the lighting to mimic evening, and the spaceships in various stages of teardown and reassembly formed hulking shadows on the floor. Unless slammed by an urgent deadline, he didn't run a late shift, so the employees had long since retired.

As he should have. He couldn't blame his insomnia on Baby. The craft had aced three more of Giorgio's test flights, performing like there'd never been a problem. He should be sleeping like an infant himself, but he'd lain awake in his quarters. Finally, he'd admitted defeat and stomped to his office. If he couldn't sleep, maybe he could work.

He'd been too antsy to do that either. Baby had provided a challenge, but not the flying-by-the-seat-of-your-pants rush he'd gotten in Cy-Ops. He hadn't realized how much he'd missed the clandestine cyborg force until last year when his buddy Kai Andros had asked for help after a mission had soured. Though he no longer worked for Cy-Ops, Dale had piloted a shuttle onto the enemy's space

43

station and rescued Kai and his protectee, Mariska. It was the most fun he'd had since he retired as a covert operative. He'd felt *alive*.

Carter Aymes, Cy-Ops director, would hire him back in a heartbeat, but he couldn't abandon the Moonbeam employees who depended on him. He'd worked damn hard to build a thriving clientele—no mean feat when you sometimes operated on the shady side of the law and couldn't advertise your services. And it wasn't like he wasn't providing *some* do-gooder service to the galaxy. Carter had hit him up for specialized vehicles several times. So had various officials of various planets. Like the Xenian emperor.

Still, he missed the euphoria of Cy-Ops, the fear and excitement merging into one glorious, powerful rush, the satisfaction of making a positive difference in the galaxy, and the pride in knowing that he and his band of cyborg brothers and sisters did what few others could do. They achieved the impossible.

As a cyberoperative, he'd extracted many individuals from sticky situations.

How was he going to extract himself from the mire of his life?

And what was he going to do about Illumina, the

real reason for his insomnia? Who was she? Why was she was here? She shouldn't have been let anywhere near Baby until those questions had been answered. But she'd fixed the craft when no one else had been able to.

He'd taken a risk hiring someone with falsified credentials, but she intrigued him like no other woman ever had. She was a riddle wrapped in mystery inside an enigma, to quote a legendary statesman. In the two weeks since she'd come on board, his preoccupation hadn't lessened, it had grown. The conflict she aroused sent his body into war.

His head argued for dismissal.

His heart whispered to hold off.

The same gut that had urged him to hire her now clenched with suspicion.

His cock hadn't swayed. It still wanted inside her.

A light flashed in the shop, and his groin tightened, sensing her presence before he detected her flowing silver hair. He'd met many beautiful women. Slept with some of them. None had provoked such a strong reaction. Why her?

And why was she wandering the shop at night?

All body parts reunified and sent his feet charging down the stairs.

* * * *

The bony protrusions where her wings used to be prickled with warning. Illumina spun around.

"What are you doing?" Dale's gaze flicked from her to the door marked *AUTHORIZED PERSONNEL ONLY*. She willed herself not to glance at the Flight Control Center and focused on his face.

"Taking a walk. I couldn't sleep." Fortunately he'd caught her *after* she'd come out of Deceptio's control room and not before.

"Is that so?" He loomed over her, and she tilted her head. His pupils dilated to obscure the green of his irises. A muscle twitched under his right eye.

"I'm not violating any rules, am I?" She clutched the lapels of her robe, resisting the temptation to let the garment slide off her shoulders. She'd given no thought to her dress—hadn't known she'd needed to as the shop should have been deserted—but had grabbed the first item handy and fled her room as if her life depended on it.

Because it did.

"You tell me." He folded his arms.

She couldn't tell him that out of her first dreamless sleep in months, she'd bolted upright, wide awake, her heart pounding with a realization of Deceptio's vulnerability. Its computer controlled the cloaking device that hid the landing strip on the moon's surface and operated the descender that allowed ships and personnel to enter the plant. With the correct secret code, *anyone* could gain entry. She wasn't safe at all! She was one hacked password away from capture.

"I decided to take a stroll," she said.

She had sprinted to the computer control room, interfaced with the network, and changed the protocol to block outside access and program a failsafe. An employee on the *inside* would have to provide the passcode. If a login attempt occurred from off moon, the system would lock down the descender and sound an alarm. Next she amended Deceptio's written operating procedures with the new instructions, sending a memo to the pilots and Flight Control as if the change had originated from Dale. The new protocol didn't make Deceptio impenetrable but much more secure. Moonbeam personnel would know someone was trying to gain entry and could mount a defense.

If Dale had been aware of the vulnerability, he would have fixed it, but that didn't mean he wanted *her* reprograming the computer without prior permission. If he learned the extent of her abilities, he'd be as likely to view her as a threat as an asset.

"Walk with me, then," he said.

What choice did she have? He gestured, and she stepped into place beside him. Constructed of sound-absorbing material, the floor muted noise. It captured their footfalls, as well, allowing them to stride quietly through the shop. Low lighting transformed the spacecraft into dark metal beasts. Together they walked from the completed area containing three ships awaiting delivery through the manufacturing area with five craft in different stages and into the parts department. Programming, including her area, Diagnostics and Repair, was located in a different part of the sublunar building.

"So why couldn't you sleep?" he asked.

"Why couldn't you?" she countered.

"I was thinking...about you."

"Me?" Her voice came out as a squeak. She cleared her throat. "What about me?"

"That's the question. What about you, Illumina?"

Her name in his rough voice sounded liked a caress. Her stomach fluttered, and that libidinous heat flooded her from the inside out. "Why are you here? What's your story?"

"I-I needed a job. I don't have a story."

"Everybody has a story."

"What's yours, then?"

He didn't speak for a long moment, and then he exhaled. "I'm a cyborg."

Of course, she knew that but couldn't say so. "Oh."

"You don't sound surprised."

Her shrug touched off a stab of pain between her shoulder blades. "I'm not," she said, trying to stick as close to the truth as possible. "You're different from most men."

"I'm not sure if that's a compliment."

"Fishing?" Despite herself, she smiled. Surely he knew he stood a head above the others. He was a powerhouse of strength and brawn. Ropy thick sinews corded his arms. Muscles flexed in a chest so broad it strained his uniforms. The rocky surface of Deceptio couldn't be any harder than his abs.

"Inquiring," he said.

"You're larger than most men I've known—bigger

than anyone here, in fact. From what I've heard"—
what she'd gleaned—"you possess a sharp mind." She
sensed a keen intelligence, human but cyber-
enhanced. He was very perceptive. She would be
smart to keep her distance.

"You flatter me," he said.

They reached his office stairs, and she expected
to take them, but he veered off down a corridor she
hadn't known about. Sensor-controlled lights
switched on. "Stating fact," she said. "How did you
become a cyborg?"

"I was an archeologist on an expedition when
Lamis-Odg attacked my team."

The terrorists. An insignificant nation-planet of
people who worshiped a mythological deity they
believed gave them the mandate to rule the galaxy.
They weren't large or powerful enough to wage an
outright war, so they resorted to guerilla attacks and
singular acts of terrorism. Their reach was spreading,
and they'd become adept at recruiting malcontents.

"They killed my four colleagues but kept me alive
in a cage not large enough to stand up in. They
smashed my legs so I could fit," he said matter-of-
factly.

Lamis-Odg had crippled him. "You were

tortured." Her throat thickened with empathy and horror. For a human, losing legs compared to a Faria losing wings.

"I survived. I was rescued and sent to a cybermed facility. Gangrene had set in, and my legs were too far gone to save. They had to amputate. Doctors offered me the option of receiving standard issue prostheses—or becoming a cyborg. It was an easy decision. Afterward, I joined...the military." He shrugged. "When my stint ended, I opened this shop."

They'd gone down the long hall, made a couple of turns, and now approached a heavy metal door. Dale palmed a scanner, and the panel slid open to reveal a personnel descender. They couldn't be going *up* to the moon's surface. So, there was another level *below*? "Where are you taking me?" she asked.

His lips twitched. "You'll see."

"Will I like it?"

"You might." He gestured.

What did that mean? His nearness had nerves buzzing with awareness. Her heart thudded. Faking calm, she stepped onto the vertical transport. "Why did you leave the military?" she asked. Keep him talking about himself, and he'd be less likely to question her. Besides, she was damn curious.

He palmed the scanner on the inside and punched a code into the keypad. Doors closed. The descender jerked and then *ascended.*

"We're going up?" Her body registered a pressure not dissimilar to the draft that pushed beneath the wings she used to have. "To what?" In hacking into Flight Control's computer, she'd discovered the factory was located a kilometer underground. Did the moon have a breathable atmosphere?

"If I tell you, it will spoil the surprise." He leaned against the wall. "Relax."

His bulk filled the space and made the enclosure seem small, tight. His warm, masculine scent seeped into the marrow of her bones. She felt light and giddy. Who needed wings when his presence made her feel as if she could fly? She focused on the fastener of his tan shirt. Metal. Round. Large and heavy. Fabricated for a big man with big hands. Would those hands be rough if he touched—

Stop it. Accompanying him had been a bad idea. She should have refused the invitation to walk. He couldn't force her to keep him company after-hours.

They rode in silence, the only noise the faint

mechanical whirring. He'd never answered her question about why he'd left the military. *This is awkward. Say something.* She lifted her gaze to his face, but he spoke first.

"Three men in my unit were killed, betrayed by an informant we'd all trusted. I'd lost the ability to disengage my emotions during missions, so I quit before my rage became a liability and I endangered my teammates.

Betrayal, she understood. Rage, too. "What *did* you do with your anger?"

"I transformed it into ambition."

"You built this shop."

"Yes."

"And that helps?"

He shrugged. "Sometimes."

An experience they shared. Without warning, defenses crashed. "My husband tried to kill me." Words she hadn't meant to say tumbled out. She began to shake.

He slapped a hand on the scanner. The transport jerked to a stop. "Is that what happened to your wings?"

She nodded. "I saw hints of anger in him before we married, but he never directed it at me." He had nicknamed her his jewel, had coddled her like a precious gem wrapped in a soft protective case. She hadn't realized when they married that the case had already become a prison. "That changed after we were bonded. When I couldn't endure his rages anymore, I attempted to annul our marriage. He intercepted me before I reached the ministry of civil affairs and tricked me into going home with him." Tears spilled over her cheeks. "H-he cut off my wings. He said he would ensure I'd never leave him again."

Dale cursed, but he was gentle as he pulled her against his hard body. His heart drummed a reassuring beat. Illumina balled her hands into fists. She'd been running for so long. His comfort coaxed her from self-imposed isolation, tempted her to lean on him and soak up the feeling of protection.

Be strong. His concern posed a hazard to her safety. His embrace, however solid seeming, was no fortress. Security was temporary at best, a dangerous illusion at worst. Nothing could prevent Alonio from finding her eventually. Her best chance for survival was to keep moving, keep him guessing.

But she couldn't resist uncurling her fists, splaying her hands over taut muscle. Dale's energy hummed against her palms. Infiltrating his computer network would take little effort, but she snapped up a barrier. She would not invade his privacy. Besides, some thoughts were better off unknown. What if he pitied her? Faria medical personnel had. She'd seen it in their eyes—heard it in their overly cheerful and loud voices, as if she'd lost her intelligence and hearing along with her wings.

"I'm so sorry," he said.

Many had offered sympathy, but few understood the trifecta of her loss: her mobility, her lifemate, her trust. All gone in a single swipe. Dale could empathize. His suffering had been no less than hers. "Thank you," she said.

"You're fortunate you survived."

"Help got to me in time." If she'd been found a minute later, she would have bled out. Illumina dashed at her wet cheeks then slid her arms around his waist and rested her head against his shoulder. One more moment then she'd move. He smelled so good.

"What happened to your husband? Did they prosecute him?" His voice rumbled against her ear.

"Questioned and released." Cleared of suspicion.

"Released?"

"He had connections." Far-reaching, powerful

ones. And when all the evidence disappeared as if it had never been...

Dale swore again.

"Thank you," she said.

"For what?"

"For caring." She let her fingertips trail over his waist as she pulled back to peer at him. His eyes were dark, intense. Conflicted.

He lifted his hand to touch her hair, stroking a long strand, letting it flow over his fingers. Warm tingles traveled up the shaft to her scalp then sizzled downward, lighting up erogenous zones along the way. Her eyes fluttered shut. *Flying again.*

"Illumina?"

Her eyes popped open.

Dale lowered his head. She met him halfway and parted her lips for his kiss. He slipped his tongue inside her mouth. Her eyes closed again, and she melted against him, her legs going boneless. They weren't in a transporter but a centrifuge that spun out inhibitions and reservations like chaff.

He'd spread his legs to compensate for their height difference, but her neck was still bent at an awkward angle. She didn't care. She needed him, this moment, this kiss. To be held. His masculine scent and taste filled her senses, seeped into the marrow of her being, whipping desire and longing into aching need.

He pulled away, his reluctance to part evident in how his lips clung to hers, by his groan. "I shouldn't do this."

"Me neither," she said, but stole another kiss.

He surrendered, hugging her tight, capturing handfuls of her hair and letting it flow like water through his grasp. Flames of lust curled, snapped, and crackled. From root to tip, her hair vibrated, sending electrical jolts zipping from nerve to nerve. Moisture pooled in her core. She was flying, careening along the edge of ecstasy. She gasped against his mouth and wrenched away. Chest heaving, she warded him off with an outstretched arm. "Stop...you almost—"

"I'm sorry. Did I tug too hard?"

"It's not that." She strove for calm and rearranged the tresses over her shoulder. Her hair did not respond to her touch the way it did to his.

"Then what is it?"

"My hair is...sensitive. With most species, the shaft part is dead. Faria hair is alive, innervated. Having you touch it like that—"

"Your hair is an erogenous zone?" A smile slid across his face.

Her hair registered tactile sensations acutely, but she'd never been brought close to orgasm by having it stroked. Only Dale's touch affected her that way. Alonio's hadn't. "Not exactly," she said, confused. Why him? Why now? On the vertical transport of all places!

With a cheeky grin, he reached out and wound a curl around his finger. Sharp sensation shot straight to her clit. She shuddered with pleasure and pulled away. "Why don't you show me what you wanted to show me?" she suggested.

A tryst with this man would be reckless and foolish. He was Terran, for goodness sake. An alien. Worse, a cyborg whose circuitry could pose problems.

He started the transporter again. Every cell of her body jittered, and her actual erogenous zones? Firing signals like mad.

Dale crossed his ankles and leaned against the wall. "So how about those Mets?"

"What?" She frowned.

"It's an old Terran saying."

"What's a met?"

He shrugged. "Some sort of a sports team. People

used to say that when a conversation got a little awkward."

Perhaps if they'd only been conversing, there would be no awkwardness. *Or if we didn't stop kissing.* Being in his arms had seemed natural, right. Not awkward at all. The situation had spiraled into something she hadn't expected. A stroll through the plant. A surprise not yet revealed—although there'd been plenty of others. Confessions. Solace. A kiss. A touch. Where did she go from here?

Away. This flirtation couldn't be allowed to continue. She couldn't start something with her *employer*. She had no energy for entanglements, even temporary ones. Deceptio provided a brief stop on a long itinerary.

With a jerk, the descender arrived at the unknown destination.

"Ready?" he asked.

"Yes." No.

The doors slid open, and the light spilled out to reveal a round indistinctive room with some low benches in the center. This was what he'd wanted to show her? There wasn't much to see. He gestured, and she ventured out.

Breathing room. Space. She expelled a sigh of

relief to be out of the confines of the transporter until its doors closed and darkness enveloped them in a tighter cocoon, heightening awareness of the *whuff* of his breath, his woodsy scent, his body heat permeating her skin no matter how far away he stood.

"Take my hand," he said, and his palm enclosed hers, fueling the riot of nervousness and desire. He guided her forward. "Sit here." He released her.

She bumped one of the benches and lowered herself to the seat. By sound, she tracked him across the room. Overhead something clicked and hummed. First a sliver then a widening expanse of twinkling light appeared. The ceiling rolled back to reveal a glass dome and a star-studded sky.

Floating center stage in the vastness—a huge orange and violet orb.

"*Naran*," he explained. "The planet around which Deceptio orbits."

"It's beautiful!" Illumina rose to her feet in awe. She'd arrived under blackout conditions so she hadn't caught so much as a glimpse of anything. On other worlds, she had seen many foreign and amazing sights, but none as spectacular as the stunning swirling lavender and reddish yellows of *Naran* looming among the stars. So expansive the view, the room seemed to spin with kaleidoscopic effect. Colors and patterns merged and shattered and reconnected anew—like her perspective, shifting and changing, forming new impressions.

I should leave.

I want to stay.

Kiss me.

Don't touch me.

"Sometimes, I need to see a bigger picture." He spoke from beside her. Enthralled by the sky, she hadn't heard him move. "That's why I had the dome installed."

"Do all employees have access to this room?"

"From the stars, they could determine the coordinates and pinpoint Deceptio's location. So, no. You're the first person to see this."

"I'm honored." Unexpected pleasure rushed through her, but so did guilt, although she'd done nothing *egregiously* wrong. Omission wasn't the same as lying, and her actual fibs were harmless, beneficial even. She'd heightened the security he so valued by reprogramming Moonbeam's entry protocol. She'd fixed his spaceship! All of that would be meaningless if she was found, but she'd be long gone before that happened, so Deceptio would be safer for her having been here.

"Is there anything on the planet?" She stepped out of his orbit, away from his disconcerting nearness, but she no longer focused on the celestial beauty, but on him. Hair endings tingled.

"No. Its surface is barren, and it has an atmosphere of poisonous gas."

"Some of the most beautiful things are toxic." Alonio was a superlatively handsome man.

Dale closed the distance. "And sometimes they're just beautiful."

How about those Mets?

Chapter Five

Illumina's hair crackled with life—or perhaps her revelations of its properties had influenced Dale's assessment. She sparkled like the constellations overhead. Her eyes radiated desire complicated by ambivalence, and if he had been a gentleman, he'd pay more attention to the latter and less to the former.

No one ever had accused a cyborg of being a gentleman.

Bringing her to his private observatory had been a whim he shouldn't have indulged. Could he trust her? Small clues pointed to no. Except, didn't everyone tell little lies? Make tiny omissions? He'd kept the observatory secret from his employees, who did not see sun or starlight for months at a time. Moonbeam bought stolen spacecraft; often sold remanufactured ships to individuals on the sketchy side of their planet's laws. His spacecraft had helped topple more than one planetary government.

So he broke a lot of rules. But, until he'd met Illumina, not personal ones.

Under the stars, bathed in Naran's glow, she was in her element as if she drew energy from starlight itself. He imagined her gliding on the wind beneath a moonlit sky on iridescent wings. How lovely she must have been. *Still was.* If he had one wish, it would be to give her wings again.

With two wishes, he would end her ex-husband's miserable existence.

He moved closer. Her eyes rounded, and her lips parted in an irresistible invitation. He ducked his head and kissed her. She stiffened but then wound her arms around his neck and melted against him. He drew her closer, showing the effect she had, and deepened the kiss.

She tasted sweet, like an intoxicating delicacy, but with the punch of *Cerinian* brandy. He could get drunk on her. Perhaps he already was. Judgment had disintegrated then balance. His head spun.

He plundered her mouth, seeking satisfaction that could only be found in deeper intimacy. He suspected getting horizontal would only increase his appetite. His cock throbbed with urgency. Never had a simple kiss turned him on to this degree. Not simple at all. Complicated.

He buried his hands in her hair, stroking from

crown to the ends tumbling below her hips. Amazing, incredible hair. Full, but as light as air, like strands of gossamer. She shuddered, moaning into his mouth.

He groaned when she slipped her hands under his shirt to splay over his back, smooth over his chest. With a delicate touch, she raked her fingernails across his skin, blazing trails of heat.

Breath mingled. Lips brushed. Tongues mated. Need rose.

Illumina broke away, her eyes molten, liquid pools. She skimmed her fingers over his shoulders to the first button of his shirt. Then the next.

He covered her hands. They could stop this now. Ride the transporter to the shop. Go their separate ways. *Think* before they acted. "Are you certain about this?"

"I'm certain about this moment."

Perhaps that was the only guarantee anyone got. Life changed without warning. When you thought you had things figured out, the world crumbled beneath your feet.

He cupped her neck, slid his hands under her robe to push the garment off her shoulders. It slithered to the floor. *Jesus, Buddha, Lao-Tzu*, she was naked underneath. Smooth, slender curves.

Small breasts tipped with rosy centers, a tiny waist flaring to narrow hips, slim legs. A nymph. A sexy siren temptress.

Faria did not blush. They silvered. They glowed. Her face grew luminous, light shining from within. She lowered her lashes in the most bashful way and proceeded to dispense with his shirt. The fastenings of his pants proved too sturdy and stubborn for her to undo, so he assisted and then they both stood nude. Stared. Admired.

"How about those Mets?" They spoke at once.

A bark of laughter burst from his throat, a giggle from hers. Awkwardness vanished under amusement before humor fell to desire.

He pressed a heated kiss to her throat, roamed his hands over parts he'd only been able to guess at. Softness registered against his palms and recorded itself in his brain and his computer network. His nanocytes snapped and sizzled.

She conducted her own exploration of his shoulders, his chest, his clenching abdomen, and his waiting cock. Without hesitancy, she grasped him in both hands, smoothing over the weeping head, the hard shaft. Her amazing hair cascaded over her shoulders to brush his skin, the lightness of the touch stirring a torrent of desire. She squeezed his balls.

"Good?" she asked.

"Sweetheart, you have no idea." He sank a hand into her hair.

She gasped. "Maybe I do."

He chuckled and then caressed her breasts, cupping each one, teasing the nipples. The curve of her waist and hips led to her mound then between her legs where he sought out feminine folds, her clit, her channel. Muscles gripped his fingers.

She continued to stroke his hard-on.

Calling to order this meeting of the mutual masturbation society. He snorted.

"What's so funny?" she asked, but she was the one with the secretive smile, pulling away, retreating out of reach.

And then she leaped. He caught her but staggered a bit, unprepared for the launch although her weight was inconsequential, her bones as fine and delicate as reeds. Her legs locked around his hips, her arms around his neck. Her wet sex lined up with the head of his cock. A perfect docking. She rubbed against him.

"Well, this is one way of doing it." He hadn't thought ahead to the mechanics or choreography, but if he had, he would have assumed they'd be *horizontal*. Stupid to assume. He'd never been intimate with a Faria before. Maybe they had sex in flight.

"I was afraid you'd want to do it in the traditional Terran manner, but that's too much pressure on my spine," she said.

"I'm guessing you're referring to the missionary position, but I don't know that I would call it traditional."

"Is this okay?"

"Perfect," he said, and kissed her. He *had* forgotten about her injury—might very well have flipped her onto her back on a bench.

She wigged and lowered herself onto his cock while he thrust upward. *Homme for the assist.* Engulfed in her tight, wet sheath, heat surrounded him, and he sucked in his breath. Yeah, standing up worked, too. Gripping her ass, he raised and lowered her while thrusting. She buried her face against his neck, licked and sucked his skin.

No hickeys.

What the hell. His nanocytes would clear up the bruising by morning before anyone saw them, maybe before they left the room. And it would be worth it.

Her mouth against his throat sent tendrils of lust curling into his abdomen. *Suck away, sweetheart.* He plunged into her then retreated. She was so slick, so warm so...he shifted her body to adjust the angle of penetration to catch her clit on the forward roll and again on the backward slide. She uttered a satisfied noise against his throat.

All righty then. He made another pass and was rewarded with another breathy moan.

All he had to do was remain upright, hang onto her, thrust, and hit all the right spots. Good thing cyborgs were multitasking masters—unless circuits got fried by an overload of pleasure.

Gripping her buttocks with one hand, he dug the other into her hair and wound it around his fist. Her pussy fluttered. Could her hair be that sensitive? He combed through the length. She gasped and clenched around him. Contractions rippled over his dick like a massage, sending pleasure rolling in a wave. His legs shook. *Oh fuck me.*

"Don't stop," she cried. Her heels thudded against his ass, and he thrust into her, doing his best to hold her and stroke her hair. Cheating—but his legs were ready to give out.

Her head fell back, and her hair dusted his

knees.

Deep in his cyberbrain, an alert blipped. *Network breached.* What the fuck? Distraction lasted for the nanosecond it took physical sensation to eradicate conscious thought. As she climaxed, her channel convulsed, milking his cock, pushing him beyond the point of no return. Orgasm loomed. Legs failed. He staggered to a bench and fell, twisting in the nick of time so that his ass hit the padded seat. A hard landing, but they maintained the connection.

He flopped onto his back. She straddled him, sitting high on his lap, her hair streaming around her. He cupped her breasts, rubbing his thumbs over the hard nipples, and then seized a handful of hair. Her face contorted with bliss.

Warning. Another ping. What the hell?

Pressure built; his cock contracted. Alerts evaporated like they'd never been. For sure, he didn't care. Caught up in the searing ecstasy, he came. Illumina cried out as she climaxed a second time.

She collapsed atop his chest. They lay there, panting like they'd run a race. Her hair covered them in a featherlight blanket. He eased his hands underneath to settle on her shoulders. "If I touch your hair, is it going to...you know?" At the ripe old age of thirty-eight, he'd thought he'd figured out the mysteries of a woman's body, but the hair thing was new.

"I don't think so." She lifted her head and smiled. "I'm good now."

After coming twice? I'd hope so. He stroked her arm from shoulder to elbow and back up. "What happens when you get a haircut?"

"Faria don't cut their hair. It grows to a natural length and stops." She ran her hand over the bristles on his head. "You cut your hair, then?"

"Yes. I keep it short. Easier that way."

She rubbed his scalp. "You don't feel anything when I do this?"

"There's a sensation," he said. He welcomed any touch from her. "It won't make me come, if that's what you're asking."

"Oh." She looked disappointed.

"Hey, you can always rub my other head."

"I'll keep that in the mind." She snuggled against his chest.

He smoothed his hands over her spine and encountered two bony protuberances covered by roughened skin. The vestiges of her wings.

She went rigid. He stilled his hands. Tactile

receptors continued to relay information to his brain. She wasn't fully healed. Perhaps would never be. She would always bear the damaged skin and hard nodules—and perhaps the scarred psyche that accompanied the maiming and attempted murder.

"The wound still pains you, doesn't it?" he asked.

"It's not so bad." She dismissed the injury but tensed like a board.

He recalled her stiff walk, her avoidance of the missionary position, how she perched on a chair edge never leaning against it. Probably her back hurt all the time.

Cybermed had achieved great strides in pain management. Doctors there might be able to alleviate her discomfort. "There are pain treatments—"

"I don't need anything. Drugs dull my senses."

He wished he could examine the scar, but she'd never go for it. "Not necessarily drugs. A computer chip might block the pain receptors—"

"I don't want to talk about this." She pushed off him, her hair tumbling forward to cover her breasts. "I'd better go. Early shift and all, you understand." He did understand. He'd literally and figuratively probed a wound, and she had bolted. Illumina couldn't have guessed how well he could see in the dark or she would have averted her backside. When she scrambled for her robe, he assessed the damage. Angry, red puckered skin stretched over hard ridges. It looked raw. He winced.

She yanked on her gown. "Um, thank you for uh...showing me the observatory." She ran for the descender.

He would have liked to have taken her to his quarters to spend the night, but that wasn't going to happen now. "I'll come down with you." He rolled to his feet.

"You don't need to do that." The vulnerable woman who'd cried in the transport, the sexy one who'd leaped into his arms and fucked like a bunny— both had disappeared. By morning, the guarded one in military dress would return. Dale didn't want that to happen. He'd always been drawn to helping the misfortunate, the defenseless, and Illumina needed him. Whether she knew it or not, whether she wanted it or not. She did.

If for nothing else than to activate the descender. "You don't have clearance to operate the transport." He pulled on his pants.

She waited, her rigid posture shouting *don't touch me*. His cybersenses picked up her fear in the pounding of her heart, her racing pulse. "Illumina..."

"Please. Let me be." She stared at the sealed exit.

After he opened the door, she entered and executed a military-sharp pivot, facing forward. He did not board, but reached in and accessed the computer with a hand swipe. "Put your hand on the scanner," he instructed her.

She glanced at him but then palmed the screen. A light blinked and then went solid. *OPERATOR ADDED* flashed.

"You can use the controls now and come to the observatory any time you wish." He stepped back, and the doors closed. The transporter whirred as it descended.

Chapter Six

"What's up?" March asked.

"I came to speak to Illumina." Her name in the gravelly tones set her heart to racing.

"Sure. She's over there."

Illumina hunched over, wishing she had a personal cloaking device. The remnants of her wings twitched as her broken body attempted to take flight. She'd spent two jumpy days peering over her shoulder expecting a confrontation. When it hadn't occurred, she'd started to relax. She should have known better. You could never let your guard down.

"Illumina," he growled. Near this time. Too near.

Gathering up the tatters of her courage, she spun around on the stool. In the observatory, it had been too dark to see, but her body had formed indelible impressions and taunted her with them now. Her hands remembered taut muscles and heated skin, her mouth recalled his heady taste, her hair tingled with memories, and her sex relived the fullness. With great willpower, she ensured none of that showed on her face. "Hello, Dale."

Everyone in the section could hear their conversation, but she had nothing to say to him so it wouldn't matter.

"We need to talk."

She jerked her head at the computer. "I'm working."

"The shift is almost over," March called. "It won't hurt if you quit a little early. You can finish up tomorrow." Damn him. Of course he would accommodate the boss.

She'd certainly been *accommodating* to the boss. Had she lost her mind? Why had she complicated an already-problematic situation? What magic had this man conjured to get her to let down her guard? He'd shown her a few stars and a planet and then she'd humped him like a short-circuiting Darius 4 pleasure android.

She could have accepted the sex part, but he'd touched old wounds, physical and psychic, and *every* shield had teetered on the verge of crashing. She wasn't prepared for the sheer naked defenselessness that flooded her. Panicked, she'd fled.

"Come to my office, please." Politeness over steel.

The normal chitchat had stopped, and a hush fell

over the room. Her fellow employees fixed on their computers, totally absorbed by their work. They were never that absorbed. *What did she do? Is she in trouble?* Of course, that's what they were thinking.

Nothing to worry about. I just fucked the boss.

If only that was the problem.

"Of course. She closed out the program and secured her terminal.

"After you." He gestured, and she had no choice but to weave through the work stations manned by exceptionally focused and quiet operators.

Once out of the section the aisle widened, and Dale assumed position alongside her.

"That was a little obvious, wasn't it?" They were out of earshot, but she kept her voice low. "People will talk." Her hair vibrated in awareness of his proximity. Memories of fusing to him like a negative ion to a positive swirled in her head. Trying not to be obvious, she edged away.

"They'll wonder why I summoned you, but if it brings you any reassurance, I don't think they'll assume we're involved. You're the only employee I've done that with."

I'm the only one? Warmth surged despite efforts to remain unmoved. "We're not involved. One encounter does not constitute involvement. " She had to disabuse him—and her stupid, yearning heart—of that notion. Another coupling could not occur. He'd gotten her to reveal too much. Worse, at the moment of climax...

"Why don't you hold your protests and arguments until we're alone?"

She tossed her head in dismissal, and a jolt of pain shot between her shoulder blades.

Her wince did not escape his sharp, cyborg eyes. "At least go to the infirmary."

"There's no need. I'm all right."

"You're stubborn."

She flexed her shoulders in defiance and veered away from the uncomfortable realization they sounded like a couple experiencing their first spat. They weren't lovers, and they had nothing to fight about. They'd had a one-night tryst. The end.

So why couldn't she forget? Why did she keep reliving the encounter? Perhaps she should be grateful he had touched her scars and brought her back to her senses, because otherwise she might have lain with him, confided more, curled up next to him as if tomorrow would never come. With little coaxing, he might make her believe in the impossible—that she could fly again. Look at how much he'd gotten her to confess in a short transport ride. She'd never intended to tell him about Alonio.

They reached the stairs, and Dale charged upward. Unable to outrun him on his own turf, she trudged after him.

His office appeared as it had the day of her interview, utilitarian but messy. She moved to the wide windows. They were tinted, and, from the shop floor, they reflected back like mirrors. From inside his lair, a panorama of the shop sprawled out. In one corner, low walls demarcated Diagnostics and Repair. She'd been smart to ask to move her workstation behind two pillars.

May as well get this over with. She turned to face him.

Dale stood on the opposite side of the too-small room, his dark eyes unreadable. He gestured to a chair piled with debris. "Do you want to sit?"

"No." She wouldn't be staying long. She twisted her hands. This was so hard.

"I would have come to speak to you sooner, but I believed you needed a few days to process what happened. I'm thinking now that was a mistake."

He shouldn't have tracked her down at all. "The

mistake was in what we did. Let's not compound it. Let's agree to go our separate ways."

"Is that what you want?" His neutral expression slipped, and she could see pain underneath. Without intending to, she'd hurt him.

"It's for the best." For him. He already cared too much. During orgasm—both of them—as she'd feared she might, she'd drifted into his head and connected with his cyber network. She hadn't intended to and she'd yanked away as soon as she could. In his headspace for the briefest of moments, it had been long enough to catch the drift of his emotions, expressed by his human side, but recorded by his microprocessor.

He cared more than he should.

She could hurt him more than she already had. She could use him for the comfort and safety he provided, mess with his emotions, and deliver the killing blow when she left. Alonio *would* kill him if he caught up with her and gathered so much as a hint they'd been intimate. From the way Dale stared at her now, it wouldn't be hard to guess.

She had to break it off permanently. A sharp pang shot through her. *This is for the best.* "What happened shouldn't have occurred, and I don't want to repeat it."

He stepped closer. Too close. She held herself rigid so she didn't sway into his arms.

"Then, I won't bother you anymore." He ran a hand over his head, and she remembered how his cropped hair had bristled again her palm. Not quite as rough, but similar, to the shadow on his jaw. Raspy. So different from her, from Faria men. "Tell me one thing," he said.

"What?"

"Your name."

"M-my name? Illumina Smith."

"Your real name."

"T-that is my real name." Alarm tumbled in her stomach. Her surname was false; her first name nearly so, although she tried to get it as authentic as she could. No direct translation from Faria to Terran existed. It was akin to translating scents into words. To describe a flower's fragrance as sweet didn't capture the smell at all. She averted her eyes from his piercing gaze.

"All right." His expression shuttered, and he assumed his place behind his desk in an obvious dismissal.

She sucked back the tears and marched out.

Behind the closed door, she sagged against the stairwell. Something *thudded* inside the office.

"Illumina," she whispered in Faria. "My name is Illumina." She shoved off from the wall and ran down the stairs as fast as her trembling legs could go.

* * * *

Dale slammed his fist on his desk. She'd walked out. Just like that. Without so much as a good-bye, see-you-around, it's-been-real. If sleeping with him had been so awful, why had she done it at all? She'd been as active a participant as he. Touching her back had upset her, but he'd assumed once she had viewed it in the context of what had occurred, she would get over it. Giving her time to think had had the opposite effect of what he'd hoped. She'd grown more certain she didn't want to see him.

She wouldn't even tell him her real name.

He had only himself to blame. Within minutes of meeting her, he'd known she was using an alias and had falsified credentials. That she turned out to be a crackerjack programmer and troubleshooter didn't count. She'd lied about everything—and he'd offered her a position anyway! What kind of an idiot hired a job applicant who lied?

Nor could he leave it there. Oh no. He had proceeded to have sex with her. "Don't fuck the staff." Wasn't that rule number one in any business?

Had her ex really attacked her or had she fabricated the tale to garner sympathy? He knew little of Faria society. Maybe they had some archaic, fundamentalist form of justice. An eye for an eye. A wing for a wing. She could be a criminal.

Her distress in the transport seemed so genuine.

However, she'd lied with a straight face at the interview. The only tell had been those flashes of luminosity.

He had a known liar working on sensitive projects. An employee who guarded as many secrets as she had access to. He should fire her, but morale and respect would plummet if word got out that they'd slept together. Had her section noticed the way he mooned over her? *This is why fucking the staff is a bad idea.*

From the stairwell outside his office wafted a song so pure and lovely, every hair on his body stood on end. His toes curled. Nanocytes vibrated. He'd never held with religion, but he could only compare the musical notes to the hallowed sound of an angel's voice.

Impossible for a Terran to vocalize.

Was Illumina singing in Faria?

Dale bolted out of his seat and flung open the door. The passage was vacant.

Chapter Seven

Hold for the monthly reports, Charlie said.

One by one, status updates pinged into Dale's head: the financials, shop safety stats, the production rotation, the spacecraft-delivery schedule, and personnel reports.

Got 'em. He opened and scanned the delivery document. Yep, Baby was on it, slated for Xenia in nine Terran solar days. Rather than send a pilot to deliver her, he would fly her himself so he could negotiate with the emperor for more ZX7Ms. Now that the bugs had been worked out, the manufacture of future ships ought to be smooth sailing.

I know you'll go through the reports on your own, but I'll highlight a few items.

His assistant was so efficient. Dale's cyberbrain processed data quickly, but he relied on the human part to make judgments about that information. Charlie saved him time by handling a lot of the minor details himself.

Charlie continued, *You'll be pleased to note we have a delivery date for the ZX7M.*

Saw that. I'm thrilled. I assume my schedule is open?

I cleared it.

Good job. Thank you. Once he'd feared Baby would never be ready to leave the nest. If not for Illumina, she likely wouldn't have.

Forget her.

Come again? Charlie asked.

Crap. He'd transmitted the thought to Charlie's computer. *Nothing.* He pinched the bridge of his nose.

Anyway, I also wanted to bring to your attention the employee leave report. The next staff shuttle departs next week.

Okay... His focus more on high level matters, he didn't concern himself with R&R requests. He scanned the monthly summaries, but supervisors coordinated staffing in their respective areas. The only employees he had to manage were his direct reports: the supervisors and Charlie.

I put myself on the shuttle, pending your approval.

Already? He frowned. He didn't begrudge Moonbeam workers time off, but routines had only returned to normal since Charlie's last R&R. *You just came back from leave, didn't you?* Three weeks and two days ago, his cyberbrain noted. The same day he'd interviewed Illumina, his human mind recalled. *Dammit.* He had to stop associating *everything* with her. Had to cease watching for a glimpse of her through the window. Quit letting her invade his thoughts. They'd slept together once. Done. Finished.

So why did he keep hoping she'd revisit the observatory? In granting her access, he'd also programmed the computer to notify him if she used the descender. She hadn't been back since that night. They hadn't spoken in the week since she'd slammed the lid on any future intimate encounters. Either she was avoiding him or she was damn lucky.

I think I mentioned my meemaw isn't doing well. She's been on my mind, and, well, I need to visit her. Just in case.

He remembered Charlie mentioning his grandmother had been ill. With Baby's delivery coming up, the timing was bad, but what could he do? *Of course you have to go.* Crap.

Thank you.

I assume Andrew will fill in again?

Not this time. He's on the shuttle, too. Regular R&R.

87

Andrew was no Charlie, but at least he was familiar with the routines.

I'll find you a good temp. Don't worry, Charlie said.

Charlie. Andrew. Dale opened the shuttle report to see who *else* was on the list he should know about. *Giorgio*. His chief test pilot. Jokester and hell-raiser. He crossed his fingers the pilot had learned his lesson after his last R&R when he'd spent most of his vacation in an alien jail after an altercation at a space casino. He continued perusing the list. Besides names, the report included the reason for the leave, such as a family emergency like Charlie's, employee illness, R&R like Giorgio's or—

Final separation. One name listed. *Illumina Smith*. He reeled like he'd been punched. She was quitting?

Why? Because they'd slept together and she found it uncomfortable to work for him? Or because he'd cranked up the awkwardness by downgrading her security clearance and ordering March to remove her from sensitive projects? He didn't *think* she'd vandalize anything, but he couldn't risk it. Her background was a tangled web of mystery and lies complicated by their indiscretion, and, until he could determine her trustworthiness, she had no business working on top secret projects. He'd been negligent to allow it.

So she was sneaking away. She hadn't had the balls to tell him to his face.

He'd never see her again.

Man, he was fucked up. She was an employee, nothing more. They'd had the proverbial one-night stand. No ties. No commitments. No promises. No morning afters. It was better for both of them that she left. He should be relieved. He wouldn't have to worry about possible sabotage or wonder what he would say if he ran into her. And he could stop hoping he would.

Boss! Are you there?

I'm here, he replied. *Sorry. What did you say?*

I said, I may not need to be gone long. If things get harried, and you can send a special charter for me, I might be able to return sooner.

Without another word, any warning, she had quit! Where would she go? Did she have another job lined up? He didn't even know her real name. He clenched his fists.

Boss?

Uh, set up whatever you want. I'll approve it.

All right. I'll keep you posted.

The second the transmission disconnected, he shot out the door. Halfway down the stairs, common sense righted itself. What the hell was he doing? He would confront her and do what? Demand an explanation? Ask her to stay? Let her tell him to his face again that sleeping with him was the biggest mistake of her life? Because hearing it was *so* pleasant the first time.

Let her go. The departure was best for both of them. He was too obsessed with her, and she was uninterested in him. He stomped to his office.

* * * *

Sweat stung his eyes as Dale pummeled the punching bag, striking hard and fast. Gloves diffused the impact, but each blow registered as a satisfying thud against his knuckles. In the wee morning hours, the employee gym was deserted. He could work out frustrations without an audience.

He'd landed another powerful blow that caused the bag to sway when his cyberbrain signaled him he had an incoming hail from Brock Mann, a former Cy-Ops teammate. He delivered another punch before tugging off his gloves and opening a channel.

Hey, he greeted his buddy.

I hope I didn't wake you. I was going to leave you a message.

Nah. I'm awake all hours these days. What did you find out? He wiped his face with a towel and tried to pretend his heart thudded from exertion and not because of what Brock might tell him.

As you suspected, Illumina Smith is a complete fiction. There is no record of anyone with that name being born on any planet. The Terran Cyberscience Institute and Infinity Corporation were hacked, the records of her enrollment and employment planted.

Of all the cyborgs, his former teammate had the most advanced computer brain. If Brock couldn't crack a code or hack into a computer, it couldn't be done. *You're sure?* He had to ask anyway.

I even searched by first name alone. Turns out it's unique. There isn't a single female in the entire galaxy with that name.

Not even Illumina herself since the name was an alias. His gut knotted. It was stupid to feel betrayed. He'd needed to cover all bases, but he'd had a good idea of the outcome when he'd asked Brock to investigate. *Well, thanks anyway. Anything on the music?*

He had converted the melody from the stairwell to light impulses and transmitted the data to Brock.

I have something for you there. It's not music. It's a Farian name.

His heart thudded against his ribs. *And?*

Faria isn't translatable into Terran or any language, but luminous spirit would be kind of close.

Nanocytes buzzed. Illumina kind of means light.

Sounds about right.

The relief...elation...that pumped through him was irrational. So, she kind of told the truth one time. Big deal. Everything out of her mouth couldn't be false. The question was what to do with the information?

Nothing. She had tendered her resignation. She still wasn't interested in him. Was leaving *him*.

Thanks. I owe you one.

I have more info for you. Your Illumina—

She's not my Illumina. He had to keep his head straight. Knowing her name didn't change anything.

All right. This person with the musical name is divorced from her lifemate. According to Farian records, an intruder broke into their residence and attacked her while her husband was away.

So her ex hadn't assaulted her at all. There you go. Another lie. When she told the truth, it was purely by accident.

However, Brock continued, I found an anomaly, some trace data that didn't fit with the official record, so I dug deeper and managed to recover a good portion of deleted code. The official record had been altered. In the early reports, her husband was implicated in the attack.

Jesus, Buddha, Lao-Tzu. She hadn't lied. So he got an official to falsify records?

I'm thinking he did it himself. Her ex is a moderately talented computer sensate.

What's that?

Basically, he has the computer capabilities of a cyborg, but without the hardwiring.

Holy shit. Ramifications rushed through his head. No wonder she had fled. If her ex had tried to kill her then expunged the records to exonerate himself, he was probably still looking for her.

A discordant static blast shot through his head, and he flinched. *What the fuck is that?*

That is the ex-husband's Farian name. I can't come up with a translation for that one, but the AOP knows him as Alonio. You can thank Pia for that tidbit. She recognized his stillvid.

Brock's wife, Penelope Isabella Aaron—Pia— served as Terran's ambassador to the Association of Planets. The alliance worked toward the betterment of the galaxy, and, since the common enemy Lamis-Odg had become more powerful, had accepted the role of interplanetary police. *He's on the AOP's most wanted list?*

Uh, no. He's Faria's AOP ambassador.

Chapter Eight

What next?

Illumina raised her face to the glass dome and studied the glittering sky. So many planets...so few options. Alonio could track her to all of them; Dale would be on none of them. Deceptio had been the safest haven, but she couldn't stay any longer.

After she'd rejected him, he'd demoted her the very next day. She still held the title and salary of Cyber Tech IV, but the work she'd been given wouldn't have challenged a Tech Assistant I. March had reassigned her, but Dale obviously had ordered it, making his feelings plain. How stupid to hope he'd approach her. Why should he? She'd only reject him again. She'd made her feelings clear, too.

Or what she needed him to think.

Until tonight she'd avoided the observatory. After all that had happened, it seemed like a violation to sneak back here, and she had assumed he had rescinded her access anyway. But as time ticked, with only a week remaining before she departed Deceptio, she wanted to see Naran one last time. The memories captured in the observatory had nothing to do with returning. To her surprise, the transporter had obeyed her command. She could have hacked in, but wouldn't have. She'd broken too many rules already.

Illumina rubbed her hands down her arms and shifted her gaze from the orange and purple planet to the bench where the beginning of the end had played out. Perhaps she'd overreacted. How could she expect to engage in sexual intercourse and *not* have him touch the scars? She hadn't expected any intimacy, physical or otherwise, so she'd been unprepared for the flood of emotion. Unable to revisit her painful loss or bear his pity, she'd pushed him away. What if she hadn't run? Would they have had sex again? Would it have become a regular occurrence?

Whooooosh. The descender whirred. The remnants of her wings twitched with an urge to take flight, but she clung to courage with resolve. The remainder of her predictably short existence would be spent on the run, but tonight she would stand her ground.

She closed the dome and switched on the lights. There would be no hiding in the dark either.

No seduction under starlight.

Yeah, like that would happen.

The transport doors slid open, and Dale stepped out. Hair endings quivered. Stomach tumbled.

He stood there silently, but the muscle twitching in his jaw said volumes. So did his clenched fists. Tension stretched like a band that could snap at any second. *Say something!* She wiped damp palms on her trousers. Any discussion would be pointless and wouldn't resolve anything. So much for the confrontation. *Coward!* Head down, she fled for the transporter. How quickly resolutions crumbled in his presence.

"You don't need to leave." His voice grated.

She stared at the doors, not at him. "I shouldn't have come."

"I meant Deceptio, not the observatory, but that, too."

"It's for the best."

"Where will you go? Do you have another job?"

"How could I? Your rules prohibit employees from accessing communication channels." She could have circumvented the block and contacted prospective employers, but the last thing she wanted was to cause a breach in Deceptio's security. And she didn't care about another job. "I'll find something."

He barred the escape route. "I spoke to March. I

had your duties reinstated."

How big of him! The force of her fury spun her around. "You felt rejected so you demoted me. Now, I'm supposed to what—be grateful you developed a conscience and opted not to abuse your authority—or is your *magnanimous gesture* your attempt at seduction?"

"No! That's not it. You're a damn good programmer."

"So you say."

"I know so."

"So I'm a good programmer, and you weren't seeking revenge. So why demote me?" The answer wouldn't change her decision, but it would be nice to know.

He looked uncomfortable. "Moonbeam's projects are sensitive. You had falsified your CV, and after what happened between us, I couldn't risk the possibility of sabotage."

She flinched. Her skin heated, and she feared that guilt glowed in her face like the luminosity suppressor had failed. She *had* tinkered with programs without authorization—had tweaked Deceptio's software to shore up security—but not out of malice. Would he understand? How could he unless she explained—and that she couldn't do.

Even if he believed her, staying posed too much of a risk. It would be only a matter of time before she succumbed to further intimacies, and that would lead to disaster.

She dropped her gaze. "I would never sabotage your shop." She moved to go around him.

"I know your ex-husband is an AOP ambassador."

His words knocked the wind from her lungs.

"That he expunged the records after he attacked you."

Her feet froze to the ground. Dale touched her arm. "He's searching for you, isn't he?"

Lies would not serve her now. "Yes," she admitted in a whisper, and then said more strongly, "That's why I must leave."

"That's why you need to stay. I can protect you."

He had no idea of the danger. Alonio was no ordinary Faria. Her chest ached. "My presence will draw him here. He always finds me."

"Because he's a computer sensate?"

"You know that, too?" She clutched at her throat. If Dale had learned so much, she hadn't covered her tracks very well, and it would be a cinch for Alonio to find her. He could be orbiting Deceptio right now, watching for an opportunity to enter. Tears welled in her eyes. It would never end, never! She stumbled to a bench and slumped onto it.

Dale sat beside her. "Let me help you."

"You can't. He has more power than you know."

"Because he's politically connected?" He snorted. "I have friends, too. Inside and outside of the Association of Planets. If you're thinking the alliance will take his side, I promise you that's not the case."

Illumina took a deep breath, and, in Faria, spoke Alonio's sacred autonym. To a non-Farian ear, it probably sounded like a staticky metal-on-metal warble.

He grimaced and rubbed his temple as if suffering a headache. "Why don't we avoid mentioning him by proper name."

No one but Faria knew sacred names. Maybe Dale did have powerful connections. "Do you understand what it means?"

"Asshole?" he guessed.

She couldn't help it, she giggled. Such mockery would infuriate Alonio. Amusement evaporated. Once, she'd laughed at a small faux pas he'd made and paid the price many times over. "It means"—she scrambled for a Terran translation that came closest—"thunder saber."

"Thunder saber?"

"He can absorb and harness energy." She held up her wrists then rubbed the right with the left.

"He shoots lasers out of his wrist?"

"He can transform his forearm into a sword."

Dale's expression turned grim. "That's how he cut off your wings, isn't it?"

"Yes."

"You don't have the ability to transform yourself?"

"No. Very, very few Faria do. It's a rare gene, and one that doesn't express itself until adulthood. I didn't learn Alonio had that ability until after we were bonded. If I stay here, he'll attack. My presence endangers you and your employees."

He regarded her with an assessing gaze. "You and he share one thing in common. You're a computer sensate, too, aren't you?"

Her jaw dropped.

"That's how you fixed Baby," he said.

She swallowed. "Yes. My gift is...um...quite advanced. It was the only reason I could stay a step ahead of him, but with his moderate ability and political connections, he's been able to find me."

Dale slapped his knees. "Here's what's going to happen. First, to put your mind at rest, let me assure you that Alonio is no threat to me. I'm a cyborg. Keeping people safe is what I do. He might succeed in drawing a little blood, but I'll wipe up the mess with his ass. Second, while I doubt he can gain access to Deceptio, as a precaution, I'll amp up security."

"About that..." She had to tell him how she'd changed the entry protocol. He wouldn't like that she'd gone behind his back. "I need to tell you..."

He held up his hand. "Let me finish. Third, *you* are not going anywhere. You're staying right here where I can protect you."

The autocratic edict set her teeth on edge. "You can't keep me here!" She hadn't fought so hard for her freedom and safety only to be dictated to by another man, however well intentioned. She was nobody's captive!

"Yes, I can."

Let him try! "As you've realized," she said, "I'm a master sensate. A computer system doesn't exist that I can't infiltrate. I can hijack one of your spaceships and be gone before you realize there was a breach. Your entry and exit protocols, for instance—"

He leaned in until his breath caressed her ear, and he whispered, "Did your orientation tour happen to include a visit to the brig?"

He was threatening to lock her up? She jerked away and rounded on him. "What are you saying?"

"Moonbeam's isolation can cause people to go a little crazy. We haven't had anyone snap yet, but the possibility exists. You could be the first ward of the Deceptio jail."

"I can access computer-controlled doors, too!" She crossed her arms.

He laughed. "You and half the employees on Deceptio—which is why they're not computer controlled." From his pocket he pulled out a metal ring and dangled some odd-shaped jagged objects. "Good old-fashioned locks and keys. The best antiques money can buy."

She leaped off the bench. "You'd imprison me?"

He rose to his feet. "In a heartbeat, if it would save your life."

He would. She could see it in the determined set of his jaw. Not a man to cross. He was a mountain. Bigger, taller, and, if his taut muscles were anything to judge by, stronger than any man she'd encountered. Only March, her supervisor, approximated his brawn, but Dale still came out ahead.

Alonio was slight but wiry and fast. He struck like lightning, inflicting thundering pain. Her wings had been gone before she'd realized his saber had been unsheathed.

Could Dale protect her from Alonio?

"My ex vowed to slay anyone who assisted me. He executed the guard outside my hospital room," she said. "Then he planted a report in the official record that a crazed patient had done it." *She* was insane for considering this. But oh, how tempting. She'd fought solo against an indomitable force for so long. "He won't stop until he destroys me."

"He'll stop." Dale flexed his fists. Had he gotten bigger? Muscles in his shoulders, his chest, his biceps bulged. His face adopted a hardness she hadn't seen before. "Because I'm going to take him out."

"Take him—"

"Kill him."

"He's an ambassador."

"He's a threat."

"There will be repercussions. Intergalactic ones."

His eyes narrowed. "Perhaps you still care for your ex-husband."

"No!" Tender emotion had been decimated long before the final attack. "Why would you say that?"

"You seem to be protesting his demise rather vehemently."

"I don't want you to put yourself at risk to save me. No one can prove what he's done. If you kill him, you'll be charged with murder. You'll be arrested."

"You don't need to worry about that."

"I do need to worry about that." This conversation was surreal. They argued about killing her ex-husband, weighing the pros and cons as if it were a debate. Alonio's viciousness had driven her to moral ambiguity.

"There's no point to arguing or worrying because this is nonnegotiable. I don't need your permission or agreement." He stalked toward her. His musculature *had* swelled and tautened. He was primed for battle.

Certainty that Alonio could prevail, *would* prevail, wavered.

"I won't allow you to leave until he is no longer a threat," Dale said. "What's it going to be? Do I put you in the brig or will you agree not to run?"

His implacable gaze reinforced his words. He would lock her up if that's what it took. That he offered a choice spoke volumes. Despite her lies and his knowledge of her abilities, he would believe her if she gave her word.

He cared enough to risk his life for her. He trusted her.

And because he did—he could. She would honor her agreement. The risks were enormous, but she would rely on her faith in him that they would win and Alonio would lose. "I promise I won't run," she said.

Dale pulled her against his chest, his arms like wings as he folded them around her. Tension dissipated, evaporating in little puffs, leaving her feeling as light as air. *Safe*. Illumina closed her eyes.

Chapter Nine

How could someone so little eat so much? Dale straddled a chair and watched Ilumina shovel through a mountain of food. He'd seen cyborgs coming off a seventy-two-hour burn not tuck away as many calories.

Perhaps as a result of the nutrition, she'd lost the gauntness that had hollowed her cheeks, but changes extended beyond that. Within a week's time, she acquired new vigor, her walk steadier, yet lighter. Her eyes weren't gray as he'd first thought, but silver, and they glittered brighter than ever. Her hair crackled with life. But the biggest difference was in her skin.

"You're glowing," he said. A compliment, yes, but also a statement of fact. It was as if every skin cell was a microscopic lantern, the combined effect of which radiated an aura of light.

"I stopped taking a luminosity suppressant." She lifted a shoulder. "Most everyone knows I'm a Faria now, so there didn't seem to be any point in hiding it."

She'd surrendered the military fatigues for silky

trousers and flowing tunics that caught the air as she walked. He loved the changes in her. He was falling *in love*.

Since their détente, they'd spent many non-working hours together, stargazing in the observatory, watching entertainment vids in the lounge, walking and talking. She'd requested a tour of the infamous brig.

He'd shown it to her.

"You really would have put me here?" She had eyed the barred cells constructed for discomfort and attitude adjustment. There were four of them, each with only enough room for a hard slab bed and a commode.

"Yes." Imprisoning her, even for her own safety, would have killed him. He would have done it—and then pummeled the gym punching bag bare knuckled until his hands were broken and bleeding.

"Hmm." Was all the comment she'd made.

"How's the training of your replacement assistant working out?" she asked now.

He sighed.

She giggled. "That bad?"

"Not terrible, exactly. She hasn't done anything major, just a lot of small stuff. Charlie is still here to catch and fix her mistakes, but I worry what'll happen when he leaves tomorrow." He rubbed the nape of his neck. "We'll work it out, I'm sure."

"You're such a good guy." She pushed her nearly empty plate away and patted her mouth with the napkin.

"What can I do? His grandmother could go like that." He snapped his fingers. "Anyway, on the positive side, I deliver Baby to Xenia in three days."

"You're taking her? Not Giorgio?"

"Giorgio will be on leave." Along with half the staff, it seemed. "I'd always planned to fly Baby. The emperor is buying her for himself. Since he's the highest ranking official on Xenia, political protocol kind of demands that the highest ranking official of Moonbeam—me—present the craft to him."

"I didn't think you cared about political etiquette."

"Usually, I don't." He grimaced. "However, delivering her gives me a chance to convince him to order an entire fleet of ZX7Ms, which is my ultimate goal. Moonbeam would be set for years."

He cocked his head. "How'd you like to go for a pre-delivery spin? I want to familiarize myself with Baby's systems before I meet with the emperor." He didn't extend the invitation lightly. If not for her, they might still be searching for the programming glitch.

Her eyes sparkled. "You mean fly? When?"

"Today. I've already cleared your absence with March."

"Yes! Yes!" She clapped her hands. "Now?" She leaped to her feet.

He chuckled. "Sure, we can go now. Let me get her prepped." Via wireless, he contacted Flight Control and ordered Baby moved to the transporter.

* * * *

Illumina at his side, Dale strolled by Charlie's desk on the way to the flight deck. His assistant and the fill-in bumped heads over the terminal. "Tap here and then toggle over to this screen and you'll be able to access the detail report," Charlie said. "Click here, key in the code I gave you, and that will transmit it to the queue in his microprocessor."

"How do I send it to his computer?"

"You *are* sending it to his computer. The microprocessor is in his brain. He's a cyborg. We've been over this." Charlie did well to not sound exasperated.

"In his brain?" Serena scrunched her forehead. If ever a person had been misnamed, she had. No serenity could be had with her around. The woman would wreak havoc the whole time Charlie was gone.

Call it callous and self-centered, but he hoped that whatever happened with the grandmother occurred fast so he could get his assistant back. "Somebody save me," he muttered.

Illumina hugged his arm. "It's not that bad," she murmured.

"Oh, yes it is."

He strode to the console, and the two looked up, Charlie squinting as if suffering a massive headache. "How's it going?" Dale asked.

"Good, I think." Serena bit her lip.

"Great!" Charlie said in the overly cheerful voice of a bald-faced liar.

"Signal for a shuttle when you're ready to come back, and I'll approve that special charter." *Please.* Thank goodness the most important project was about complete. He couldn't risk Serena dealing with anything regarding Baby.

"Will do, thanks."

"I'm taking Baby for a run. If something comes up, ping me."

"Check," Charlie said.

"You have a child?" Serena asked.

Shoot me.

"The ZX7M," the three of them said together.

"Oh, yeah. You mentioned that."

"Several times," Charlie muttered.

"How many grandmothers do you have?" Dale hoped he didn't have to suffer through this again.

Charlie frowned. "Just the one..."

"Shouldn't we go?" Illumina nudged his arm.

"Yeah," he agreed through gritted teeth. Because otherwise he might strangle Serena or Charlie or both of them. How could there be such a disconnect between Serena's supervisor's assessment and her abilities? Her boss who'd volunteered her services had raved about her capabilities. Unfortunately, there wasn't time to train anyone else.

"Give her a chance; she's probably nervous," Illumina whispered as they walked away.

"I'm trying." What was being tried was his patience. He thought he gave employees a fair shake, but could he be the problem? Cyborgs intimidated some people, and he hadn't bothered to hide his impatience and irritation with her mistakes.

Frustration melted away when they climbed into

the cockpit of the ZX7M, and Illumina's face lit up with a radiant smile. He folded himself into the pilot's chair and motioned her into the co-pilot's. They strapped in.

Dale switched the controls to voice so Illumina could follow along. "Flight Control, this is Homme, authorization Yankee Papa nine eight nine. Activate descender."

"Roger, Homme."

A minor jolt, and then the craft lifted off the shop floor as the vertical transporter pushed it upward. Baby rose into the shaft that led to Deceptio's surface. The granite of the moon's upper crust replaced the view of the manufacturing plant. As they rose, the cockpit pressurized.

Atop Deceptio's day-lit surface, moonscape barren of all but sand and rock spread over a desolate, dull-gray plain. The runway stretched long and clear, the crawling maintenance bots having removed debris blown in by the eddies. "Computer! Ignite engines and prepare for liftoff."

"Acknowledged."

The floor vibrated as the engines fired.

"Activating thrusters. Prepare for lift-off in ten, nine..."

At the count of one, the thrusters roared and engines spun with a high frequency, near-inaudible whine, shooting Baby down the runway like a bat out of hell. Moonscape blurred, and then she climbed into the sky. The steepness of the angle put them at a recline. He glanced at Illumina to ensure she was okay and not in any pain. "All right?"

"I'm fine," she replied, but there was a slight tightness around her mouth.

They reached the moon's outer atmosphere, and Baby leveled out. Below, through the view screen, the runway and descender pad shimmered and then winked out of view. "It's gone!" Illumina gasped.

"That's the cloaking device at work," he explained. "Not only is the landing strip invisible to the eye, but the computer can't see it either. To land on Deceptio, you need the exact coordinates or the device needs to be turned off."

If someone happened to be orbiting Deceptio when someone entered or left, they'd see the runway. Still, he'd have to be in the right place at the right time. If an intruder landed, he couldn't operate the descender without the password and a link to the central computer. The vehicle transporter could lower only one ship at a time, eliminating the possibly of a massive invasion. If an enemy managed to get into the plant, he'd be a sitting duck on the dock, outmanned and outgunned. Dale's cache of arms was second only to Cy-Ops's arsenal. With the security redundancies, no place in the galaxy was more protected than Deceptio.

"How many people have the coordinates?" she asked.

"Only a handful with a need-to-know." He reached over and squeezed her hand in reassurance.

They cleared Deceptio's thin atmosphere, and Dale grabbed the stick. "Computer, switch auto control to manual."

"Acknowledged. Switching in five, four, three..."

He zoomed Baby closer to the vividly orange and purple Naran but remained clear of its gravitational pull.

"It's more beautiful here than through the observatory," she said. "Not inhabitable, you said?"

"No, and that's good for us. That means that there's no reason for someone to come to this section of the galaxy." It made Deceptio the perfect place to hide a spacecraft chop shop—or a Faria on the run.

"You thought of everything."

"I tried to. Do you want to see more of Naran or

see how fast Baby can go?"

"Fast, please!"

He veered away from the planet and opened up the throttle. Baby responded immediately, hurtling through space. Through the side viewing windows, stars streaked by. He glanced at Illumina. She radiated a silver aura, her smile glowing all the way up to her sparkling eyes.

He tipped Baby's wings, rocking the craft from side to side. Illumina giggled, her laughter tinkling like bells. Dale grinned and guided Baby through another minor acrobatic maneuver, banking her left then right.

Probably the Xenians would disapprove that he'd taken their craft for a joy flight, but fuck 'em. The computer would record the flight hours and maneuvers, but the use could be chalked up to a final test. His shop had built the craft, he was the boss, and what the Xenians didn't know wouldn't hurt them. Breaking his own rules mattered little if it meant seeing Illumina happy.

"You want to try a loop?" he asked her.

"Yes!"

He lifted the nose in a positive pitch urging Baby into a climb. At the top of the loop, she flew upside down. Illumina squealed. Only their harnesses kept them in their seats. Illumina's hair cascaded downward like an electrified waterfall.

Baby followed the circle 360 degrees around.

One more maneuver and he'd call it quits. Dale guided the craft into a vertical figure eight. Musical peals of enjoyment had him chuckling like a mischievous kid. But his body reacted like a man's. Desire surged in a wave of heat.

He eased back and trimmed the speed to a cruise.

"That's going to have to be it," he said. The craft *did* belong to the Xenians, and he didn't want to press his advantage too far. Besides, he wasn't some horny sixteen-year-old trying to impress a girl in hopes of getting laid.

I'm a horny thirty-eight-year-old....

"Can I fly it?" Illumina looked at him, her expression pleading.

"You know how?"

"You grip the stick, right?"

Grip the stick. He had a stick—shit. Keep it in your pants, Homme.

He put his raging hormones on hold to focus on the request. There was no reason why she couldn't take the controls for a bit. They weren't navigating through an asteroid belt or launching or landing. The ZX7M was gliding through open space. She couldn't hit anything. Even under manual control, Baby practically flew herself. If Illumina stalled the craft, it would just float—and he'd be right here. Hell, if not for her, Baby would have been grounded.

"All right. Keep it level. *No rolls or loops,* okay?"

"No rolls or loops, I promise."

She grasped the controls on the copilot's side, and he let go of the captain's. She sat straight in her chair, her gaze shifting from the instruments to the viewing window. The seriousness of her expression made him want to laugh. "You can open up the throttle a little," he said.

Baby shot through the sky like she'd been catapulted.

"A little!" He started to grab the stick but caught himself and gripped his seat edge instead.

"Sorry." She grinned but eased up on the speed.

They cruised through the blackness bejeweled by dazzling stars. Other than Baby's throaty hum, there was a companionable silence, seductive in its intimacy. It teased more than his body. It kindled a yearning for a partner to walk the walk. *This is what it could be like if you had someone.*

Not just anyone. Her.

He'd imposed his will, forced Illumina to remain on Deceptio for her own good, but by all indications, she'd accepted moon arrest, had relaxed and thrived. Would she consider staying once the threat no longer existed? Or would she fly away? Once she had her freedom again, would he lose her?

He'd find out soon enough. He'd called his former boss Carter Aymes and got Cy-Ops working on the ex-husband problem. Before much longer, the ambassador would become a notation in the history annals. As a cyberoperative, Dale had committed his share of assassinations for the betterment of the galaxy, but he'd never *ordered* a hit before.

His conscience didn't bother him in the least. If he had any regrets, it was that he couldn't do the honors himself. He needed to stick close to Illumina. He disliked leaving her even for a couple of days, so he'd enlisted March as backup beginning with his upcoming absence from the plant and until Cy-Ops neutralized the threat. March, a cyborg, was a former Cy-Ops teammate. Carter had volunteered a third cyberoperative as an additional bodyguard. The odds were infinitesimally slim that anyone could breach the moon's defenses, but if someone did, he'd never get past three cyborgs. He wouldn't get past the first one. Alonio would meet his deserving end.

Dale scrutinized Illumina sitting in the copilot's chair, her face alight with joy. Thanks to her miserable ex, this was the closest she'd get to flying.

Her gaze met his. "Thank you for this," she said.

"You're welcome."

"We should head back, huh?"

"Yeah. You want to turn her around and take her to Deceptio?"

"Aye aye, captain."

When the moon appeared, stark and gray in the distance, he switched to autopilot, and Illumina released the controls.

"Computer, prepare to land, set coordinates to five zero by nine six," he instructed.

"*No landing strip detected at those coordinates*," the computer said. The cloaking device hid the runway from the ZX7M's scanner.

"Override. Whiskey tango. Nine nine."

"Override accepted."

"We won't be able to see the runway until we're almost on top of it," he told Illumina. "Under normal operating procedure, I'd tap into Flight Control's computer and switch off the cloaking device, but given our current scenario, I want it in force as much as possible. After touchdown, I'll transmit the descender activation password."

"You're not going to contact Flight Control and have them do it from the inside?"

"No, there's no need."

"Uh…" She expelled an audible breath. "I have something to tell you. I, um, changed the protocol in Moonbeam's computer. Flight Control has to activate the transporter. Moonbeam's computer won't respond to a command from a ship on the surface or in orbit."

"What?" Dale scowled, not liking what he was hearing. "When did you do that?"

She twisted her hands. "The night…the night you showed me the observatory."

"When I found you outside Flight Control."

"I should have mentioned it sooner."

"You think? Why did you do that? My pilots are no security risk. They've been vetted, and I trust them. After we land, you and I need to have a discussion." He couldn't allow her to bypass his authority. If she'd been anyone else, he would have fired her on the spot.

"While the codes are being transmitted, a sensate could intercept the password."

The meaning sank in and settled in the pit of his stomach like a rock. He'd locked the door but left a window open. Not only could a sensate intercept the codes, a cyborg probably could, too. She shouldn't have hacked into the system without his permission, but she'd found a serious security loophole. He should have realized and addressed the vulnerability—and not just because Illumina had been threatened.

"Besides reprogramming the system so that the descender can only be activated by an insider, I rewrote the operating procedures and sent out a memo under your name."

Baby dove through Deceptio's atmosphere. "*Prepare for landing,*" the computer announced. Not until the craft had lowered the landing gear did the runway become visible.

The craft touched down with a small bump and glided down the strip. As it slowed and taxied to the descender, he contacted Flight Control per Illumina's new procedures. The craft sank beneath the moon's surface, and they were encased by rock and silence.

"You're mad at me, aren't you?" she said in small

voice.

"No." Yes. More at himself for failing to notice Deceptio's vulnerability. She had overstepped her bounds, but had been motivated by self-defense, not malice. Protecting her was his number one priority. And, in truth, she'd made Deceptio safer for everyone. He unclipped his harness and twisted in his seat. Sparkling silver eyes had dulled to a worried gray. Dale cupped her nape. "No, I'm not angry," he said, and meant it this time. "The fix needed to be done. I should have caught it. Before you do anything else, ask me—or at least tell me."

"I promise. I really am sorry."

"It's okay." He caressed her cheek. Her skin felt like silk, such a contrast to his. He'd been a field operative in a paramilitary organization. They wore protective gear when possible, but sometimes you didn't wait to suit up, you jumped in and did what needed doing. His robotic nanocytes repaired much of the damage he inflicted upon himself, but his body had paid the toll. He did not have a prissy official's hands, nor an *ambassador's*, but a fighter's. Scarred, callused, rough. With those hands, he'd keep her safe.

He brushed her cheek then couldn't resist stroking her hair. It crackled, and Illumina parted her lips.

"I want to kiss you," he said. *Tell me no.* If she didn't want this, she had to be the strong one because, around her, his good intentions evaporated faster than his willpower. He'd vowed to keep their relationship professional, but one smile, a laugh, a glance, a descender ride, and promises crumbled. What was it about a vertical transport that led to thoughts of getting horizontal?

"What are you waiting for?"

Good sense maybe? *That* would be a long wait.

With a groan, he covered her lips. He explored her mouth, coaxing, forcing lightness as need stormed through him. Illumina teased back, sucking his bottom lip, nipping at it.

Baby continued her measured descent to the shop floor, but he was freefalling. He grabbed for the buckle of Illumina's harness, unsnapped it, and pulled her onto his lap. Kissed her as if that alone could sate his desire. Of course, it couldn't. Each caress, each touch deepened the hunger.

He fondled her neck, her arm, the curve of her waist and hip, before settling on her breast and thrumming the nipple. With a moan, she arched into his palm.

The pulse in her throat replicated his own fast beat. Baby would pop into view in the shop in a few moments. Fortunately, his cyberbrain kept track of details when his human mind got distracted. He kissed her and grabbed her lustrous hair. She gasped into his mouth.

He leaned his forehead against hers. "You make it hard to resist you."

She chuckled, her breath mingling with his in a mix of sweetness and desire. "You're not supposed to resist me."

Caving to the craving had not gone well the last time. An interlude of ecstasy had led to flight, avoidance, estrangement. If he pursued her now, would the same thing occur? They'd reached a level of understanding and fledgling trust, but could respect and mutual regard lead them through the hazards? His raging boner urged a hasty decision, but he'd been down that road and didn't care to walk it again.

"I don't want to resist you," he said. "I'd prefer to carry you to my quarters, get naked, and fuck until we both pass out—but I would like you to be there when I wake up."

Her face flashed with a guilty luminescence. "I

will be." She undid the fastening of his shirt. "Promise."

He would have sworn he'd heard a choir of angels sing. "All right then." A hard kiss sealed the deal, and he deposited her in the copilot's seat and redid his shirt.

The descender delivered Baby to the plant safe and sound then rotated so she faced nose out. A dolly towed her off the lift so that the landing bridge could attach to her starboard side. In the hours they'd been gone, the work shift had ended. Other than the skeleton crew operating the docking tool, the factory floor was vacant. Thank goodness. He hadn't looked forward to leading the march across the high bay with a stiffy.

It was bad enough the test-flight supervisor waited at the end of the dock. "How did it go?" he asked.

"Flew like a dream," Dale said, relieved Illumina stood in front of him and hid his arousal from view. "The Xenians will be thrilled."

"Good." The supervisor signaled his crew. "You can move her out, guys!" The flight area was kept clear for exiting or returning spaceships. None were expected this evening, but procedures were no good unless they were followed.

"Well, good night." He nudged Illumina, and they hurried away.

Chapter Ten

Sensor-controlled lights flickered on as Dale shouldered into his private quarters. Illumina glanced around, eager to learn more about the man as revealed by his personal space. His sitting area accommodated a replica of the sofas in the employee lounge, except longer, so he could stretch out, no doubt. Through an open door, she spied his bed, no different from the bunks in the barracks, only larger, with its thermal cover wadded into a ball at the foot. She stifled a grin at the idea of him on a standard bunk. His knees would dangle over the edge.

"If I'd expected company, I would have picked up a little." A faint blush tinted his cheeks as he kicked a pair of boots underneath a table, grabbed an armload of clothing, and tossed it into the adjacent bedroom, and slammed the door. With a wry grimace, he ran a hand over his head.

They'd be entering that room, too. She swiped a hand over her grin, charmed by his nervousness.

"Can I get you a drink? Cerinian brandy?" he asked.

"That would be nice. Thank you." She figured he needed it as much as she did.

While he got the brandy, she examined a group of stillvids on a credenza. A smiling couple held two small children, the boy she recognized as a younger, mischievous version of the man getting brandy. "You look the same," she said. "Only...more."

He snorted and uncorked a bottle of amber liquid. The second image showed a mature Dale with four other men, three of them as big and muscular as he, one startling familiar. Her gaze shot to Dale.

"Buddies," he answered her unspoken question. "Kai Andros, Brock Mann, Carter Aymes"—he poured two shots—"and March you already know." He brought the drink over to her.

"You knew March before you opened the shop?"

"We go back a ways."

She eyed the stillvid, realization dawning. "You're all cyborgs?"

He nodded. "Except for the guy in the middle. Carter. You'll meet him tomorrow."

Carter stood as tall as the other men but couldn't match their physique, their musculature.

She set down the stillvid to accept the small glass. They clinked. Dale downed his in a single gulp, while she took a tiny taste. Fire seared her throat, bringing tears to her eyes. "Oh hell!" She coughed.

"Sorry." He grinned. "I should have warned you. Cerinian brandy doesn't affect cyborgs."

"Potent stuff," she said, and shifted her gaze to the third stillvid. Dale and two men and two women knelt over a dusty pile of rocks, purple sky behind them. "Friends?"

"My archeology team."

"The ones who were killed." After which he'd been captured and tortured.

"Yeah."

"Again, I'm sorry."

"Thank you."

She braced herself and sipped her brandy, managing not to choke this time. She studied his Spartan accommodations furnished in a minimalist manner. "Your place says a lot about you."

"That I'm boring and utilitarian?"

"That you're a fair man. You don't take advantage of your position. You're living pretty much like the employees who work for you."

"I do have my own private ChemShower," he joked, but a trace of red darkened his cheekbones.

"And you did take a client's spaceship for a joy

flight." She finished off the brandy.

"Just to impress a girl. See? I'm a terrible human being."

She set her glass alongside his on the credenza and slid both hands up his chest. "It worked. The girl is impressed. Thank you for that." She rose on tiptoe. He met her halfway in a searing kiss.

Jolts of desire skipped from the top of her head to the soles of her feet. Heat settled low in her belly. He dragged his lips to her ear. His breath, warm and gentle, evoked a strong shudder.

His jaw rasped, tantalizingly prickly. She rubbed her face against its abrasiveness then sought his mouth again. After a deep kiss, she pulled away. "Why don't you show me the rest of your quarters?"

"Okay, but you have to promise not to look too closely. It's kind of messy."

"Don't worry. I'll focus on you." She would. The last sexual encounter had come as a surprise. She hadn't expected to become intimate that night and had rushed away afterward. There would be no rushing of any kind this time.

He closed his palm around hers in a warm, secure grip. Everything about this man appeared larger than life—his hands, his height, the breadth of his shoulders, his muscles, and his—yeah, that part, too. She dropped her gaze to the bulge in his trousers. Yep, just the way she remembered.

"Like what you see?" he asked.

Her turn to blush, but she boldly replied, "Looks promising."

He pulled her close for another kiss. "I always keep my promises."

Lights blazed as they entered the tiny bedroom dominated by the large bed. "Computer, dim illumination by 80 percent," he said, and kicked the heap of clothing into a pile in the corner.

Illumina's lips twitched. "Are you dousing the lights so I can't see the mess?"

"Oh, you're funny," he said, but his amused expression turned serious, and he trailed a fingertip from her temple to her jaw. "And beautiful."

Her wings had been beautiful, eliciting compliments from envious Faria. Shimmering and translucent, they had appeared as delicate as gossamer but had been as strong as tree limbs swaying in the wind. How fast she'd flown! After they'd been cut from her body, the stumps had shriveled and curled to unsightly lumps. She'd never considered herself vain but she hated for him to see the ugliness.

Her expression must have revealed something of her thoughts because his eyes darkened. "Are you sure about this? We don't have to."

The other time had occurred under the cover of darkness. The lights were low now but bright enough to reveal her injury. What if the scars repulsed him? If they proceeded to make love, how would that affect the future? Would this be the start of something—or the end?

Confidence wobbled, and she didn't like it.

She disliked the fearful, hesitant person she'd become. She'd fled from evil; she would not run from good. She wanted him; she needed this. If she ran, it would be toward Dale, not away from him.

Begin as you mean to go on. "I want to." She spread her hands over his hard chest. His heart thumped, and his scent rose to tease her senses, the merest whiff coaxing her closer.

He stroked his knuckles along her cheek, catching threads of her hair, sending a shiver along her nerves. Her hair had always been sensitive, but never so much as with him. Only he affected her like this, the slightest touch kindling hot tingles and deep yearning. She'd never imagined herself with an alien, part man/part machine, but, here and now, she'd couldn't envision being with anyone but him. *My cyborg.*

He brushed his mouth over her lips in a light caress. She clutched his shirt and deepened the kiss, needing more. He gave it to her with a growl. His erection twitched against her. Slow caresses turned fervent. Between kissing and groping, clothing, his and hers, joined the heap on the floor.

He was more powerful naked than clothed. His legs were long and stout, not weak like hers. Corded muscles bulged in his arms. Dark curly hair matted his massive chest, arrowing down a ripped abdomen to a nest around the base of his thick erection. Her core fluttered.

"Are you checking me out?" he asked.

She lifted her gaze. "I did promise to ignore the room."

"Let me show you the bed at least." He pointed. "Bed."

"Noted," she replied, smiling.

They stretched out side by side, face-to-face. Mouths fused and tongues mated in a sexual fury, but his hands were gentle as he roamed them over her body, finding and igniting hotspots. He fondled her

135

throat, her breasts, her tummy, between her legs, the backs of her knees. Every touch deepened the hunger for that final completion.

From scalp to tip, he combed his fingers through her hair, and she shook with need for him.

"Are you cold?"

"No." She grasped his cock, stroking its length. Body hair teased her nipples as she scooted down to take him in her mouth, to tease him until he shuddered the way she did. She sucked and laved his erection, swiping her tongue across the head, drawing him as deep as she could then pulling back with a long, slow drag.

"*Jesus, Buddha, Lao-Tzu!*" He growled some foreign words she had no translation for. But the meaning was as clear as the ache in her center, as the urgency that spiked when he threaded his fingers in her hair. Heady, mind-spinning pleasure climbed to a crescendo.

He pulled her on top of him.

She wrestled away.

Confusion knit his face.

Illumina stretched out onto her back. Pain jabbed at her spine, but she ignored it and reached for him.

136

Bewilderment cleared from his expression, but he held back. "What about your...injury?"

"It will be fine." The pressure against scarred nubby bone felt like jagged rocks, but she wanted him on top, craved his possession in this way.

"Try this." He grabbed a couple of the pillows they'd kicked to the floor. He flattened them out with a punch. "Lie on these."

She raised up so he could position one under each shoulder blade lifting her spine from the bed, and she relaxed. Better. Not totally pain free, but better.

"Okay?" He leaned over her.

She wound her arms around his neck. "Perfect," she lied.

With a little jockeying, he found his place between her thighs. She locked her heels against his buttocks, and his erection nudged her. With a push, he breached her entrance and rocked inside. Despite the twinges in her back, satisfaction filled her as deeply as his cock, and she released her breath with a hiss. If she'd had wings, she would have wrapped them around them both. She moaned and clung to him, her body moving, encouraging his thrusts.

He kept his weight off her torso, bracing himself

on his elbows. Veins pulsed in his temples, his throat, and face as their bodies slid together. He twisted fistfuls of her hair, sending tendrils of piercing rapture careening through her body, driving her to desperate heights. She clasped his neck, digging her fingers into taut muscle.

Mind and body separated, her psyche soaring on wings of ecstasy. She flew, unfettered and free, as waves lifted her up, up, up. Her pussy contracted around him, igniting more jet streams of pleasure.

Dale groaned. *Need her. Want her. Love...oh fuck...*His thoughts flowed into her consciousness. She jerked, and he did, too, going wide-eyed before he grimaced, plunging deep, his cock convulsing and releasing. His spasmodic tugs on her hair sent her spiraling again.

Passion spent, she lay beneath him. *I did it again. Glided right into his head.* Maybe the violation hadn't registered. He'd been *preoccupied*, on the verge of orgasm. He hadn't said anything about it but panted against her neck, his breath steamy.

He pressed a kiss to her throat then lifted up and rolled off. "Are you okay? I didn't crush you did I? How's your back?" He eyed her, his expression concerned.

Whew. She surreptitiously pressed her thumb and pinky finger together in a Farian gesture of thankfulness. "I'm fine," she said.

His scrutiny turned calculating. "You really are a computer sensate, aren't you?"

Fuck, she swore silently. Profanity didn't exist in the Farian language, so she stole a curse from his. "I'm sorry. I didn't mean to. It was an accident."

"It happened the last time, too, didn't it?"

Miserable, she nodded. "I hoped I could control it. I assumed because I wasn't mentally prepared before... I'm sorry." She rolled over to get out of bed.

He grabbed her wrist. "What are you doing?"

"Going to my quarters. You have a right to be angry because I invaded your privacy."

"I'm not mad." He hadn't released her, leaving her no choice but to lie beside him. After hooking the thermal cover with his toe and pulling it over them, he faced her, his hand beneath his head. "I'm not mad, but I am going to have to watch my thoughts. What if I'd been thinking, gee, she looks like she put on a few kilos?"

She gasped. "You-you—"

He laughed. "I'm kidding. Trying to lighten the

mood." He tugged on a lock of her hair, and sensation coiled between her legs. It would be wise to never tell him how strongly playing with her hair affected her.

He squinted like he had a headache. "Can you tell what I'm thinking now?"

She shook her head.

"You're not getting any thoughts or images of purple cats?"

"It doesn't work that way."

"How does it work?"

"I'm a *computer* sensate. I can't read your human mind, but I can tap into computer software, and since you're a cyborg…"

"You have access to what my microprocessor records."

"I don't do it deliberately. I try to avoid it, actually. But, during strong emotion, when my barriers crash, it sort of happens. I have to be touching you, though." She had to physically connect with a computer system to integrate into it. That was the way her gift had always worked.

"Has it happened with anyone else?"

"No. You're the only cyborg I've been with." And the second man ever.

"So it didn't happen with…?"

"Not in that way."

He frowned. "Not in that way? What does that mean?"

"Alonio and I had been matched as lifemates, and when we joined in marriage, we formed a psychic bond that forged an awareness of the other even when we're apart."

"Wait a minute—"

"I severed the bonds," she added. "The lifemate connection enabled him to hunt me down when I first left him. It also allowed me to sense when he was around so I was able to escape. Every time he found me, I identified and broke the psychic threads. I think they're all gone now."

"You think?" He pulled back.

"He found me within a matter of days the other times. I've been here about a month. That he hasn't shown up and I haven't sensed him at all, are good signs." She sought to reassure him.

"How long were you on run before you came here?"

"About two months. The first time, he found me two days later. I had to flee the hospital." Still in critical condition, nowhere near healed, leaving the infirmary had jeopardized her life, but staying would have ended it for sure. Alonio would have killed her in her bed. "Gradually, it has taken longer and longer for him to find me."

"How long was the previous longest stretch?"

"A week."

He relaxed with a sigh. "So a month is a good sign. Probably you have cut the ties, but with this new information, I'm glad I called for reinforcements." He pulled her against his chest, and she tucked her head on his shoulder. His heart thumped comfortingly and she snuggled close.

He caressed her arm. "Now, back to us...when did you realize you could get in my head?"

"When we were intimate in the observatory." She bit her lip. "I got a hint at the interview. When we shook hands, I sensed I might be able to connect to your processor."

"Huh."

He seemed to be taking the news well. She scanned his face. "Why aren't you angry?"

He tucked a strand of hair behind her ear, sending a zing zipping along her nerves. "I'm used to communicating via wireless with other cyborgs. It's almost like telepathy. So having you listen in when we're having sex isn't that unsettling." He grinned.

142

"Besides, I doubt that you'll pick up anything more interesting than, *Fuck, I'm going to come,* but now that I know you have this ability, I'll erect a firewall to keep you from gleaning any deep, dark secrets." He glanced at her. "No offense."

None taken. Instead, a load of guilt lifted off her shoulders. "Do you have deep, dark secrets?" she teased.

"Two or three. You already know one of them."

"And what's that?"

"How much I like you."

Yeah, she'd caught the drift. "I-I like you, too."

"Care to test it?"

"Test it?" she asked then felt his cock twitch against her leg. "Ah, you mean the firewall. Maybe we should. Just to be sure." She smiled and traced the arrow of hair down his abdomen.

He was right. When she spiraled to the height of rapture and her consciousness connected with his microprocessor, the only thought she picked up from him was, *Oh fuck, I'm going to come.*

Chapter Eleven

The Terran's shoulders twitched, and then he scratched his nose, signaling the computer had dealt him a good hand. The other players folded. Dismay and anger flitted across his face like a vid reel. If anyone should have avoided gambling, it was the Terran. He had so many tells, everyone in the gaming hall knew what kind of hand he had. Alonio almost felt sorry for the pathetic loser.

A gag-inducing stench reminiscent of rocket exhaust wafted into the room several long seconds before the *Barbadian* henchman-for-hire sauntered in. Drool dribbled down two tusks protruding from his mouth. His bulk blocked the entrance as he scanned the crowd. When his gaze alighted on the Terran, he grunted.

"Perfect," Alonio murmured. He couldn't have asked for better luck.

The Barbadian loomed over his quarry. "Mr. Jennetta would like to speak to you," he growled.

"I'm in the middle of something right now." The Terran shifted on the stool and looked to the other gamblers with a beseeching expression, but they had eyes only for their gambling screens. The android game monitor turned his back. *See no evil.* No one wanted to tangle with a Barbadian.

With a chortle of satisfaction, Alonio crossed his arms. If he had planned this, things couldn't have gone better.

"Now." The Barbadian grabbed the Terran's arm and yanked him off the stool.

"Well, all right. All you had to do was ask."

"This way." The henchman jerked his head toward the exit, flinging a string of mucous spittle onto his captive's shirt.

Disgusting. Alonio glanced at his pristine white suit and shuddered. He'd have to be sure to stay out of range. When the right time came. For now, his best strategy was to let the situation ride.

The Terran nodded, and the two started to weave through the gaming cubbies. They'd taken a half dozen steps when the Terran broke away and ran. The alien bounty hunter caught him by the scruff of the neck and hauled him kicking and blubbering out of the hall.

Alonio smoothed the sleeves of his suit and slipped into the vacated chair. "May I join you gentlemen and lady?" He guessed the noseless, earless creature with facial horns was female.

"You got the credits, you can play," the monitor bot said.

He tapped into his screen and sent five hundred thousand credits to the android. Linking his consciousness to the computer, he altered the gaming code. After three rounds, which he won, he decided the Barbadian had had enough time. He cashed out his winnings, wished his companions luck, and departed.

The henchman's body odor and his quarry's screaming led him to a back corridor of the casino, deserted except for a few android service workers who weren't programmed to care that a man writhed on the ground, clutching a dislocated shoulder.

"I have the credits, I swear!" the Terran cried. "Let me go to Exchange, and I'll transfer them to Mr. Jennetta's account. I was on my way—"

"You have one million credits?" the Barbadian scoffed.

"One million? I only owe Mr. Jennetta half a million."

"That was last week."

"Please..."

"Enough!" The alien henchman hauled him up and swung him by his bad arm. The Terran screamed.

This was too easy. Alonio allowed the Terran to dangle in agony and terror while he adjusted the lapels of his jacket then he lifted into the air and glided down the corridor to land beside the two men. He folded his wings to his body. When pulled tight, they resembled two swords mounted against his back.

The Barbadian dropped the Terran into a heap. "What do you want?" he snarled. His breath smelled as bad as his body odor.

"Gentlemen," Alonio said, though neither was, "I confess I overheard part of your conversation and believe I may be of assistance."

"This isn't your concern." The henchman spit, and the noxious glob landed on the toe of Alonio's white boot.

His arm tingled from elbow to fingertip, but he smiled through the rage. The Barbadian deserved to die, but killing him wouldn't make his case with the Terran, and, unfortunately, he needed the sniveling coward's assistance.

"He's going to kill me!" the Terran blubbered. "He wants money that I don't—that he won't give me time to get—"

The Barbadian kicked him. "Silence, you useless sack of excrement!"

"Now, nobody's going to kill anybody. Not when we can settle this like gentlemen." He unclipped his Personal Communication Device from his belt and tapped into his account. "Allow me to cover his debts. One million, payable to Mr. Christopher Jennetta, correct?" Alonio already knew the particulars, having researched the situation prior to selecting the Terran.

"Thank you, thank you," the Terran sobbed.

The Barbadian scowled. "As I said, this isn't your business. I don't have authorization to deal, and Mr. Jennetta insists on seeing him." He yanked the Terran to his feet. The man emitted a piercing girly scream.

The Terran shrieked again when Alonio marshaled his energy and, in a burst of flame and light, transformed his right forearm into a sword.

"Perhaps I could convince you that it is in your best interests to accept the credits on Mr. Jennetta's behalf," he said in a soft voice.

The Barbadian didn't flinch but he eyed the saber. "I might be able to talk to Mr. Jennetta—if you care to make it worth my while."

Captured by the Cyborg

There was no requirement to offer the Barbadian anything. One swipe of the sword would end this discussion, but he admired a man who stood his ground, a man who stood for *something*, not like the cowering Earth alien who'd wet his pants. A million credits. Five hundred million. A billion. Credits meant nothing when you were born into one of the wealthiest families on Faria.

"One mil to Mr. Jennetta and another mil to you, perhaps?"

"Deal." The Barbadian grinned, his yellowed, dirty teeth revealing the source of his halitosis.

Sword became flesh again. "Your name, sir?"

"Harber."

Using his PerComm, he transferred one million credits to Jennetta and another million to Harber. "Done."

The Barbadian eyed Alonio's sword arm before saluting with a small wave. "Pleasure doing business with you." He sauntered away.

The Terran shuddered. "Thank you. I owe you my life. You saved me. I promise I'll repay every centicredit—"

"I don't want your money. I have no use for it." Alonio waved away the offer.

The man gazed at him with something akin to hero worship. And more than a little lust. This wasn't the first time he'd attracted a male's interest. Among the peoples of the galaxy, the Faria were considered the most attractive, and Alonio bore no modesty, false or otherwise, about his exceptional looks.

"Are you all right?" He gazed into the Terran's eyes and flashed him a calm, concerned smile. "He didn't hurt you, did he?"

"M-my arm," the Terran said. It hung crookedly from the shoulder.

"May I examine you?"

"All right."

He probed the Terran's dislocated shoulder. "I think we can fix—" He snapped the joint back into place.

The Terran yelped and grabbed his arm, but then his expression relaxed. "It's better!"

"Glad I could help." He focused on radiating reassurance to camouflage his disgust. He preferred the malodorous Barbadian over this creature. The henchman had been right. The Terran was a sack of excrement. But a useful sack of excrement.

"Look, Mr.—"

"Alonio."

"Mr. Alonio. I owe you my life. I want to repay—"

His body humming with energy, he stepped back and released his sword again, holding it high and turning it so that the blade caught the light with a beautiful and deadly gleam. An awesome force of nature. The Terran fell back, his gaze riveted on the sword with equal parts fear and fascination. Alonio itched to do the galaxy a favor by ridding it of this pathetic wretch, but that wasn't why he'd come. The sorry excuse for a life-form could provide him with something he needed.

He transformed the saber back into flesh and bone. "If you would be so kind, there is a *small* matter you could help me with."

* * * *

"Dale—Sonny Masters. Sonny, this is Dale Homme." Carter Aymes, Cyber Operations director conducted the introductions.

"Nice to meet you. Thanks for coming." Dale sized up Sonny. The dude could be mistaken for a thug. Injuries pre-dating his transformation to cyborg marked his face. A scar zigzagged from his left eye to chin, and his nose appeared to have been broken more than once. Nanocytes, if injected promptly, could repair or reverse many injuries, but not those sustained years prior.

"Happy to help out a fellow cyborg." Sonny's perma-glower vanished under a warm, lopsided smile.

"Quite an impressive installation and operation you have here." Carter nodded approvingly as the three men descended the dock. The director whistled through his teeth as he spotted Baby sitting pretty, ready for delivery later that afternoon. "Wow."

"That's why I called for backup." Dale ran a hand across his head and looked at Carter. "If I was dealing with a civilian customer, any of my pilots could deliver Ba-the ZX7M. However, this is Xenia's emperor, and I have to personally present it to him. We've been working toward this for months, but the timing could be better."

"From what I can see, your security is rock solid—literally," Carter said.

"I'd like to think so, but more is at stake than proprietary technology. I won't take any chances with her life."

"She'll be safe," Sonny said. "I'll guard her with *my* life."

"I know you will." He slapped the other cyborg's back. No one wanted to die, and avoiding it was generally the plan, but each and every Cyber Operative would defend his or her protectee with his or her life. They would throw themselves on a microexplosive device if they had to.

"Holy crap, is that what I think it is?" Carter gaped at a Lamis-Odg military ship.

He grinned. "Yep."

"How the hell did you get that—no, don't tell me. It's better if I don't know."

"Don't ask. Don't tell," Dale quipped.

Chattering in their native language, two Arcanian techs in coveralls rushed by them. One of them bumped Carter as he passed. "Excuse, excuse," he muttered, darting away with his companion.

"Hold it!" Dale ordered.

The two workers froze.

He glowered at the one whose six eyes blinked at different intervals. "Whatever you stole, Jesse, give it back."

Jesse glanced at his companion then sighed and slipped a webbed hand into his pocket and extracted an expensive-looking universal tool.

"What the hell?" Carter snatched the gadget.

Dale crossed his arms. "All of it."

His expression sheepish, the Arcanian produced a titanium Terran United presidential medallion, which had been awarded to Carter's now-deceased father. On the secret interplanetary market, the metal alone would net a pretty sum.

"Get back to work," Dale snapped.

Jesse and his co-worker made themselves scarce.

"Sorry about that," he said.

"Son of a bitch." Carter pocketed the items. "That's it? He robbed me, and all you say to him is 'get back to work'?

Dale shrugged. "Thievery is almost a genetic compulsion with Arcanians. I think their brains are hardwired that way. They're good employees, but I do regular pat downs and searches of their quarters to recover *lost* objects."

"They sound like they're more trouble than they're worth," Sonny growled.

"Most people think so, which is why almost no one will hire them."

"Why is that one named Jesse? That's not an Arcanian name."

"No. Another employee who's a history buff nicknamed him. Jesse James was a notorious bank robber centuries ago."

"I've never heard of him," Carter commented, "but it sounds appropriate."

"Come on, I'll introduce you to Illumina before I head out." He'd held off delivering Baby until Carter and Sonny could arrive.

"How much does she know?" the director asked.

"She understands I'm a cyborg, that I used to work with other cyborgs, and that I've called in some friends, but I didn't tell her about the organization."

"Good."

"Any progress on the objective?" he asked, although he guessed the answer. If the target had been neutralized, Carter would have said so by now.

The director compressed his lips. "Not yet, but we'll get him. He's a bit wilier than we expected. We get a lead, but he vanishes before we get there. The assumption is that since he's a moderate-level sensate, he's planted tracking cookies that tip him off, so we flooded the cybernet with false trails to confuse him.

"We restored most of the deleted files about the attack and forwarded them to the AOP. The Alliance has initiated an investigation. There's an interplanetary warrant out for his arrest."

Dale hoped Cy-Ops got to Alonio before the AOP. Either way, justice would prevail, but he preferred it to be the swift and decisive cyborg kind and not dragged out for years by bureaucratic red tape.

Ping! A hail from Charlie's PerComm shot into his brain.

Hey, boss! I'm ready to return to work if you'll a send a ship.

Thank goodness! Only two days had passed since his assistant's departure, but he didn't think he could endure another hour of Serena's assistance and had concerns about how she would handle matters in his and Charlie's absence. Twice she'd deleted important transmissions, and he had to call in tech support to retrieve them. With Charlie to lend a hand to Carter and Sonny, Dale had one less worry on his mind. *You contacted me in time. I think I can catch the regular shuttle on its return sweep. It's picking up Giorgio anyway.*

So soon? Why? What happened?

He didn't say. Just that his R&R plans had fallen through.

Hope he's not in trouble this time.

Me, too, Dale said. Work hard, play hard. Sometimes Giorgio played too hard. If the pilot had

157

fucked up again, he'd be on his own. He had more important things to worry about than a space jockey who loved to raise hell as much as he loved to fly. *Can you get to the drop-off planet?*

I'm already there.

He tagged a pickup ticket priority and shot it to the employee shuttle coordinator and asked Charlie, *What's the news on your grandmother?*

Meemaw surprised us all. She rallied and pulled out of it. She's tough.

Good to hear. I have to leave to deliver Baby to Xenia, but I already alerted the shuttle coordinator.

Thanks, boss.

March will be in charge while I'm gone, and a couple of buddies of mine, Carter Aymes and Sonny Masters, are visiting Moonbeam. Take care of them, will you?

You bet.

They disconnected the transmission.

"Problems?" Carter asked.

"What makes you say that?"

"I've been around cyborgs enough to recognize the look."

"Actually, it's good. My assistant Charlie has been on leave. He'll arrive tomorrow. If either of you need anything, he's your go-to person. He practically runs this place." He beckoned with a wave. "Let's go to my office. I'll have March and Illumina meet us there," he said, and messaged the other cyborg.

Be there in a few, March replied.

Upstairs, the two men admired the bird's-eye view through the window. "You get a chance to fly most of those craft?" Sonny asked.

He thought of his joy flight with Illumina. "A few." To rib Carter, he said to Sonny, "If you get tired of making nice-nice with terrorists and criminals in the galaxy, I'd be happy to put you to work as a test pilot."

"Yeah?" Sonny said.

"Fuck off, Homme." Carter glowered.

Dale and Sonny laughed. All three men watched as March and Illumina strode across the shop floor. Actually, all eyes were on her. His included.

She was beautiful. And tiny compared to the cyborg. Was that how they looked together? A giant and a fragile sprite. She glanced up at the window and stared right at Dale as if she could see through the glass, although the two-way mirror prevented it.

March said something to her, she laughed, and Dale's stomach tightened. *It doesn't mean anything.*

What do you expect, she can only laugh with you? Awareness of the irrational nature of his jealousy didn't eliminate it.

"She's pretty," Carter commented, making it worse.

Just pretty? A bizarre tangle of emotion shot through him—another surge of jealousy that the director thought she was attractive—and a contrary annoyance that he didn't notice that she wasn't pretty, she was beautiful. "Yeah, she is," he bit out.

Moments later, March and Illumina entered.

"Hey!" March and Carter greeted each other with back-slapping hugs. Handshakes ensued between March and Sonny.

"A pleasure to meet you." Sonny's grin transformed his face from thug-like to charming.

Carter shook her hand. "I've heard a lot about you."

"I recognized you from your stillvid," she replied.

Eyebrows arched, Carter glanced at Dale.

"Team shot," he said, unable to message the director that Cy-Ops's secrets were secure. Carter had founded the covert paramilitary organization, but he wasn't a cyborg.

Dale wished he didn't have to leave, but Illumina

would be well-protected, and the sooner he left, the sooner he could return.

"How long will you be gone?" March asked.

"Two to four days."

"That long?" Illumina's face crinkled with dismay, but she straightened her shoulders. "Never mind. You need to do what you need to do. I'll be fine."

Now he really wished he didn't have to go. "You'll be safe. I have total confidence in these guys."

She flicked her gaze to the other men before glancing at Dale. "It's not that. I'll miss you, that's all."

How many more reasons could there be for not going? He hoped the Xenian emperor wasn't given to a lot of pomp and ritual. Dammit. "I'll miss you, too," he said huskily.

She lit up with a silver glow, and his body responded, his groin tightening with an ache. The flight to Xenia would be long and hellacious. But, as soon as he landed back on Deceptio, he'd get Illumina naked. Maybe they'd revisit the observatory—

The three men peered intently out the window at the shop. Damn the lack of privacy. Dale shot Illumina a rueful smile then cleared his throat.

"Here's the plan. Carter will use my office as a command post to continue the cyber search for Alonio. March will continue his supervisory duties in Diagnostics and Repair, which will enable him to keep watch during work hours. At night, Sonny, you're on. I've put you in the barracks nearest Illumina's room. Deceptio is as secure as it can possibly be, so within the facility she's free to come and go as she pleases." He paused and sought her gaze, "You need to keep March, Sonny, or Carter apprised of your whereabouts."

She nodded.

"Are we expecting any arrivals or departures of craft or personnel?" March asked.

"Just the returning employee shuttle. Charlie and Giorgio will be on it."

"Why didn't you put a moratorium on shuttle flights while you were gone?" Carter asked.

"My assistant had a family emergency. Some of the others had had their R&R booked for months. I couldn't approve his leave and cancel the others without a mutiny." He was just glad Illumina had stayed on Deceptio. Not that she'd had a choice. He would have locked her up.

"Don't you have to lower the shield?"

"Lowering the cloaking device does create a moment of vulnerability, but we've never had a breach during five years of operation."

"How many entries and exits have you had during that time?" Sonny asked.

He queried his database. "Eight hundred sixty-eight."

"That sounds like a lot," Carter said.

"Well, each entry also means there's an exit and vice versa. We've purchased or traded for ninety-two vehicles which we refurbished or tore down for parts to produce sixty-one craft delivered to the buyers. Add to that 152 test flights, sixty employee shuttles, forty special charters, and twenty-nine unplanned arrivals."

Carter frowned. "Like what? What kind of unscheduled visits?"

"Such as Kai Andros who arrived on the run from Lamis-Odg. All people I know and trust."

"If you factor exits and entries, the length of time the cloaking device is shut down and allow for spacecraft traffic in the area, the chance of infiltration or penetration is less than one-tenth of one percent." The statistical odds were on his side, and he felt confident Deceptio was impregnable, otherwise he would never have considered leaving Illumina. Life rarely offered certainties, but, with March and Sonny both watching over her, her safety was as close to guaranteed as he could get.

Still, Alonio needed to be neutralized ASAP. He couldn't keep her under moon arrest forever, and if the meeting with the emperor resulted in a contract for a fleet of ZX7Ms, flights to and from Deceptio would increase significantly. New staff would have to be hired. The cloaking device would be down more often. The more successful and profitable Moonbeam became, the harder it would be to maintain security.

"I expect business as usual while I'm gone. I left a message for Charlie that March is in charge. Feel free to call on my assistant for anything. He's here to help." He rubbed his hands together. "That's it. Any more questions?"

"No." The men shook their heads.

"No," Illumina said. She'd been quiet during the debriefing.

He hoped she wasn't afraid. "Everything will be fine. These guys will take good care of you," he said again.

The men nodded.

"I know," she said.

"Walk me out?" A kiss wouldn't be enough to sustain him, but it would have to do.

She nodded solemnly.

"I'll go down with you, too," March said.

Dammit. So much for being alone.

"Sonny and I will remain here and set up shop," Carter said.

Thank goodness for small favors, anyway. "Sounds good. Serena will be up later to show you to your quarters." Charlie's fill-in could handle that much. Maybe.

Illumina giggled.

Carter and Sonny exchanged a frown. "That's funny because?" Carter asked.

"She's"—he struggled to find a tactful word—"new."

"I'll see that they get to the right place," March offered.

"Thanks," he said. Many people approached cyborgs warily, not quite sure how to pigeonhole them. Were they human? Android? He tended to forget what it was like to be *only* human. So Serena's exceptional incompetence might be due to nervousness—and he had to admit he hadn't been as patient as he could have been. But, if recent work performance was close to her norm, her employment needed to be reconsidered.

A hell of a realization now that he had to leave. "Keep an eye on her, too, would you?" Dale said.

Carter arched an eyebrow. "Problem?"

It was that the one-tenth of one percent probability again. No, no problem. Most likely. "Don't give her anything taxing or classified. By tomorrow, Charlie will be back."

"Great. Well, I'd better get a move on. Thanks again for coming." He slapped Carter on the back and shook Sonny's hand then he, March, and Illumina left the office.

In the stairwell he gestured to March. "You go on ahead."

"All right. Have a safe trip. Sell lots of ships and don't worry about anything here. We've got it covered."

March disappeared, and Illumina flew into his arms. "I thought he'd never leave."

He chuckled and kissed her, inhaling her scent, savoring her taste. What began as a slow good-bye turned frantic, lips and teeth colliding, tongues lashing as if the separation of a few days meant forever. He disliked leaving her at this juncture, but she would be fine. He'd be gone four days tops. Security couldn't get any tighter. All bases had been covered. So where was the desperation coming from? She felt it, too, clinging to him and winding her arms around his neck in a near chokehold.

If he acted concerned, she would become needlessly worried. "Think about me while I'm gone," he said.

"I'll think about nothing else."

"Good." Gently, he tucked a strand of her hair behind her ear. "I'll be thinking about you."

"Even when you're negotiating with the emperor?"

"Especially then."

"Right. I believe that."

"Honest. 'Hurry up, Your Emperorness, and make a decision.' That's what I plan to tell him."

Her tinkling laugh filled the stairwell. "I believe the proper address is Your Majesty."

"Whatever." Dale laid another lip-lock on her. "I won't be gone long. I have a girl waiting for me."

She drew back, silver eyes serious. "I'm your girl?"

Yeah, she was. For no other reason would he have put so much effort into ensuring her safety. He hadn't needed to deal with the situation himself. As soon as he'd learned of the danger, he could have passed her off to Cy-Ops. Eliminating threats and protecting the vulnerable was what they did all the time. Hell, it was their mission. In their protective custody, she would have been safe and secure.

But she would not have been with him, so he'd used the potential danger as an excuse to keep her near. Hell, he'd coerced her compliance by threatening to lock her up in the brig.

Not very honorable.

She still stared. An indication he'd probably misread the depth of her feelings. He didn't doubt she was attracted to him, but sex didn't have to mean anything. Maybe she'd been making the best of a bad situation. Separation might provide some clarity. She could discover how she felt, and he, well, he already knew how he felt. He could get a grip.

"We'll talk when I get back. You'll have time to mull it over." He turned to descend the stairs.

She barred his path and planted her hands on his chest. "You surprised me, that's all. So you'd be like my a...a...boyfriend? Is that the right Terran word?"

A silly term from long ago for which no better word had ever been coined. "Yes."

"I've never had a boyfriend before." She smiled. "I would like that."

"Well, good." His face could crack he was grinning so hard. He hadn't felt this giddy when he was sixteen. "You've *never* had a boyfriend?"

She shook her head. "We don't date since Farian marriages are arranged."

Somebody had set her up with that monster. *Don't think about that. Not now. There's nothing you can do, and it will make you crazy.* They had so much to talk about, and he had to leave. He planted another hard kiss on her mouth. "When I get back, we'll talk." After they humped like bunnies.

He took her hand, and they descended the stairs.

Chapter Twelve

Buzz.

Illumina jackknifed out of a dead sleep. Muscles between her shoulder blades spasmed. Fear clawed at her throat, cutting off air. *Run! Get out!*

She leaped out of bed. Her legs tangled in the thermal blanket, and she fell, hitting the floor with a light thud. Her heart pounded, and her breath came in gasps. *It's okay. It's okay.* She strove for calm and to free herself from the blanket. The danger signals sizzling through her brain weren't real.

Buzz. When the saber had sliced through the air and cut off her wings, there'd been no sound, not even a whisper.

Buzz!

What was that? *Buzz!* She jerked her head at the harsh sound, and her gaze landed on the wall scanner. *BUZZ.* The volume increased, and the screen flashed, lighting up the room like a strobe.

The scanner. No danger. Just the scanner. She pressed a hand to her thudding heart, dragged in a lungful of air, and stumbled across the room. She palmed the screen and swiped the comm link. "Y-yes?"

"Did I wake you?"

Thoughts fuzzy, she recognized the pleasant male voice, but couldn't place it. "Um...yeah. Kind of." Simulated morning lights weren't on yet. She squinted at the screen. Two a.m.

"Sorry," he said with an apologetic laugh. "I thought you'd want to know Dale is arriving."

Sleepiness vanished. "When?"

"Now. His craft is on the runway. Should be just a few minutes, if you want to come meet him."

"Yes, I would. Thank you for waking me." She tried not to sound too eager, to be discreet, for all the good it did. Word must have gotten out that they had more than an employer-worker relationship or she wouldn't have gotten a wake-up in the wee hours of the morning.

She'd missed her cyborg like crazy. The two days he'd been gone had dragged. "I'll be right out." She disconnected the comm line and activated the lights.

Heart still racing, but with excitement now, she rubbed her eyes. She shrugged out of her night robe and pulled on a lavender gown that enhanced the color of her hair and eyes. She wanted to look good for the reunion.

Work had kept her busy during the day, but the evening hours were long and lonely.

With any luck, the visit with the Xenians had proven productive and a contract for more ZX7Ms had been secured. She hoped Dale's feelings hadn't cooled during the separation. Before he'd left, they'd reached a turning point in their relationship, and he'd promised a discussion when he returned.

Action first. Talk later. Desire and longing pulsed. The night terror that had awakened her faded into nothingness.

Her hair hummed as she brushed it with a bristled desensitizer allowing her to smooth it out without discomfort. Dale always seemed entranced by her hair, like it was something unique. Men! She didn't understand his attraction to it, but it pleased her that it pleased him. She arranged the silvery tresses over her shoulders and back then eased her feet into a pair of slippers and hurried from the dorm.

Lights, tripped by sensors, came on as she skipped along the hall. She slowed as she passed Sonny's room. Wake him?

Negative, as the men would say in their military way of speaking. If they hadn't already been called, she wasn't going to do it. She'd agreed to keep her bodyguards apprised of her whereabouts, but Dale had returned so their responsibility had ended. Besides which, she did not wish for company. The men would find it impossible to resist debriefing each other and alone time would be delayed by hours.

Under the reduced lighting in the high bay, spacecraft loomed like sleeping giants. Her footfalls made soft *pffts* as she trod across the floor. She eyed the office overlooking the entire operation. Was Carter up there? The man was tireless. He wasn't a cyborg, but he had the determination and fortitude of one. He'd been excited yesterday, reporting he'd gotten a lead on Alonio's whereabouts. Soon, he'd promised her, her ex would be a non-issue. She could not fathom what that would be like. To never have to hide or run again. To be free to just *be*.

She owed it all to Dale, Carter, Sonny, and March. The men belonged to a military organization of some sort. They hadn't said, but their camaraderie, precision, and attention to detail spoke of it. AOP? Possibly, but probably not. If they'd been with the Association of Planets' peacekeeping battalion, they would have said so. AOP operated openly. She'd bet her credits the men belonged to a clandestine paramilitary force of cyborgs. She would ask Dale. Probably they had taken some oath of confidentiality, but if she'd already guessed...maybe he would confirm it.

Pillow talk for later. First, she would hustle him to his quarters, strip off his flight uniform, and show him how much she missed him.

She picked up the pace and skirted around a hulking, menacing-looking Lamis-Odg military craft.

And ran into Carter.

"It's late," he said. "Why are you in the high bay? Where's Sonny? Did you notify him you'd left your quarters?"

She stifled a curse. "No, I didn't see the need—"

He shook his head. "Are you kidding me?"

"Because Dale is back."

"He's on site?" Carter frowned. "I wasn't notified."

"I was. His shuttle has arrived."

Carter's hand went to his PerComm.

"What are you doing?" she asked.

"Notifying March and Sonny."

Great. One interloper wasn't enough. Now she had a welcoming *committee*.

"Who called you?" Carter looked up.

"Charlie." She sighed. As her head had cleared of sleep, she'd been able to place the caller.

Carter relaxed, tension easing from his body, and he reclipped the PerComm to his belt. "Don't suppose there's a need to wake them now. Morning will be soon enough."

"I would think so," she said, relieved.

"Come on. Let's go meet the craft."

Not as bad as an entire party, but not optimal. "All right." She tried to pass off a grimace as a smile.

"I won't keep him long."

She smiled for real this time. "Thank you."

They strolled among the spacecraft, heading for the docks.

"I continue to be impressed by the factory," Carter said.

"Haven't you purchased ships from him?"

"A few." He nodded. "I hadn't visited the plant before. He had the ships delivered."

He'd never been to the factory. Hmm. Nobody had explained Carter and Dale's relationship sufficiently. Dale had called him a "buddy," but, while they were cordial, they hadn't acted like friends. Did he know him from the military? Carter looked more like an administrator than a soldier. Yet, he'd shown up when Dale had hired an extra bodyguard for her. She took a stab at the truth: "How long did Dale work for you in your secret cyborg organization?"

"I don't know what you're talking about." He lied without missing a beat.

She wasn't deterred. "I didn't fall off a supply ship yesterday," she scoffed. "I see the similarities between Dale, March, and Sonny. They're built like soldiers or warriors. They share a connection. And then there's you. When Dale needed assistance, you came, too. But you're not a cyborg." She eyed him. "My guess? You lead the organization they all belong to."

"I can see where you might draw that conclusion, but you're wrong."

"Fine." She shrugged. It had been worth a shot. She'd work on Dale. *After I work on Dale.*

They arrived as the docking bridge rolled toward a gunmetal-gray power craft. Overheads spotlighted the operation.

Excitement fluttered in her stomach, and Illumina fidgeted. She wanted to race up the steps and fling open the spacecraft hatch herself but had to wait until the disembarkation apparatus had been attached. Damn, it was slow. Hair endings tingled.

Soon, very soon. They just had to get rid of Carter. She glanced at him.

He furrowed his forehead. "Didn't another pilot go with him to fly him back?"

"That's the standard procedure with deliveries."

"Is that the shuttle the pilot took?"

She'd walked Dale to the landing area. Watched as he boarded Baby and then disappeared in the vertical transport. She hadn't stuck around to see what pilot boarded what craft to follow him. "I guess so."

The dock tool attached to the ship.

"I watched both of them leave. This doesn't look like the same shuttle."

"Maybe he traded with the Xenians. He exchanges spacecraft all the time," she said, only half listening. Dale was back!

Docking complete, the hatch rose with a hiss. She darted for the stairs.

"Illumina, wait a second," Carter called.

She ignored him and sprinted up the steps. The hatch folded against the hull. "I'm so glad you're back," she cried. "I missed you!"

Clad in white, Alonio stepped onto the dock. He stretched his silver wings. "I've missed you, too, wife."

Chapter Thirteen

Illumina screamed. She vaulted down the stairs, leaping two at a time, tripping over the last three. She hit the ground face down and skidded across the polished floor.

"Motherfucker!" Carter lunged forward and yanked her to her feet. "Go! Get Sonny!" He shoved her and ripped off his PerComm.

She ran. The bay darkened under a shadow. Alonio landed in front of her and folded his wings to his back. His hands hung relaxed. "It's time for you to come home."

Icy terror seized her throat. He wouldn't bring her "home." He would kill her. She could read his intention in his sociopathic gaze.

"You're under arrest!" Carter pushed in front of her.

Alonio's perfect lips twitched. "You have a protector. How...charming." A blinding flash of light exploded.

When her vision returned, Carter's severed left arm lay on the shop floor. With his right hand, he clutched at his ragged shoulder, blood spurting like a geyser, his expression dazed, disbelieving. His mouth worked, but no sound came out.

A saber glinted from Alonio's right forearm.

"No! Stop it! No!" she cried.

With a lightning-fast strike, Alonio opened up Carter's right leg near the groin.

Carter screamed.

"Stop!" She charged, striking with her fists. He grabbed her hair and wrenched her to her knees. Carter's blood soaked through her clothing.

Another swipe took off Carter's leg at the hip. He collapsed, unconscious.

The saber shifted into a dagger. Pain stabbed into her head in a starburst of agony as Alonio sawed through her hair and tossed the skein of silver onto the floor.

He yanked her to her feet and pressed the knife to her throat.

Footsteps thudded across the high bay. March appeared. He leveled a blaster. "Release her."

"I don't think so. Drop your weapon, or she dies now."

Alonio would kill her and them. He wouldn't hesitate. *Do as he says, please do it,* she tried to communicate with her eyes. March shimmered in and out, vision clouded by pain and tears. She didn't dare speak, afraid any movement would give cause to slit her throat.

"Then I'll kill you," March said.

"Perhaps," Alonio conceded. "But she'll still be dead. Is this what you want?" He jerked his head at the body on the floor and then drew the tip of the blade across her neck. Pain lanced her throat. Warmth trickled down her chest. Blood.

March bent at the knees and set the blaster carefully on the floor.

"Over here," Alonio motioned.

His expression grim, March gave the weapon a shove. It slid across the floor.

Alonio whipped around. Dagger transformed into a saber that he drove into Sonny's abdomen as the cyborg lunged from the shadows.

"No!" Everything she had feared would occur had come to pass.

Sonny grabbed for the saber, but Alonio retracted it with a twist, spinning around to swipe at March who'd charged. The cyborg leaped back in time to avoid being gutted. Sonny, his face contorted, sank to his knees. Blood darkened his uniform, spilled through his fingers pressed to his abdomen. Blood, blood, everywhere. On Carter's body, on Sonny, on her, splattered on Alonio, spreading across the floor.

Saber became a knife that pressed against her throat again. Alonio gripped her waist and held her tight. He lifted off, his wings slicing through the air. He landed on the dock, and hauled her toward the waiting spacecraft.

She gaped at the carnage. Sonny critically, possibly fatally injured. Carter dead. March, in vain, trying to resuscitate him.

"You! What are you doing there?" Alonio rounded on an Arcanian crouched at the hatch. Knife became saber again.

The tech scrambled to his feet. "Excuse. Excuse. Flight Control instruct. Say ensure dock release from craft," he mumbled in broken Terran.

"Get out of here!"

Four of the Arcanian's six eyes focused on Alonio's face; the other two stared at the saber.

"Go! What are you waiting for?"

The worker darted forward, but stumbled as he drew abreast. "Excuse. Excuse." He found his footing and fled in fear.

Alonio dragged her into the craft. After closing the hatch, he dragged her onto the bridge, and sealed the cockpit.

Tears streaked her face. "You didn't need to kill them." Carter and Sonny had become casualties because of her. She never should have stopped running. Dale had believed he could protect her, but he couldn't. His team of cyborgs couldn't. No one could.

"I told you I would kill anyone who helped you." He assumed the pilot's seat and grimaced as he noticed the bloody splatters staining his sleeve and trouser legs.

"Why? Why can't you let me go?" She eyed the cockpit scanner. She could integrate into the computer system and unlock the seal—but not fast enough to evade the light saber.

"Because I love you."

She choked. The madness that consumed him wasn't love.

He tapped into a screen. "Flight Control, diplomatic charter 179 is ready to depart."

"Roger that. Prepare for disengagement." Charlie's voice!

Dale's assistant had let Alonio in. He'd had been

on leave when the employees had been debriefed. In his haste to get to Xenia and back, Dale must not have thought to alert him, and who would think an AOP ambassador, a diplomat with perfect credentials would be a threat?

But, why would *Charlie* be in Flight Control at all?

The truth sank in. "What did you threaten Charlie with to get him to help you?"

"You know I never threaten, my dear. Have I not made good on everything I told you I would do?" The craft rocked as the dock maneuvered out of the way. "The young man offered to assist after I helped him out of a jam."

She could only imagine what that might have been. Charlie must have been desperate, or Alonio had made him so. She eyed her ex with loathing. He'd fooled so many people.

Once again, it was just her and him. Where would he take her? Not to Faria or anyplace civilized. Maybe he had a personal torture chamber on some off-the-grid planet. That would bring his sadistic heart the most pleasure.

Bile rose in her throat, and she forced it back. She had to concentrate, but spikes of pain hammered into her scalp with the slightest movement. The ends of her hair throbbed like raw, exposed nerves.

Her wings.

Her hair.

He intended to destroy her piece by piece. The best she could hope for was a quick death. "Why don't you kill me now?" she said. "You know you're going to."

"Because that would be too easy."

She lunged for the scanner. Her palm slid across the screen. Codes to open the door skidded through her mind, but before she could grasp the final number, Alonio spun her away. He wasn't a big man, but he was wiry, lithe, and in perfect form. He struck her across the face, snapping her head, wrenching her neck. The returning backhand sent her careening across the bridge to smash into the piloting console. She lay gasping, blood streaming from her split lip.

Dale, help me. In her mind, she cried out. She would never see her big cyborg again. Her chance of happiness, gone, stolen along with her life. Hatred simmered.

"Sit down," he ordered, as if she was acting like a lazy, disobedient child for slumping atop on the console. Her head wobbled, too heavy for her neck.

Gray dots danced in front of her eyes.

The ship rotated as the spinner underneath turned toward the descender. The slight rocking sent hair endings into agony. Her entire body spasmed with pain.

She dragged a hand across the console smearing blood on dials and gauges.

"I won't tell you again. Sit down."

Illumina planted her palm against the screen and pushed herself up. On her feet, she swayed, still clearing her head of everything extraneous. Time flowed in slow motion. One...two...threeee...

He moved toward her, and she dropped into the copilot's chair.

A tow dolly guided the craft into the transporter, which lifted them to the moon's surface.

* * * *

Dale's microprocessor ordered a regiment of nanocytes to lower his heart rate and pulse. He schooled his features into a blank expression. "Forty-five billion IP credits for forty ships, delivered at a rate of eight per annum," he deadpanned, his voice absent of the urgency zipping along neural pathways.

He wanted this contract, but he needed to wrap up negotiations so he could get back to Illumina.

The Xenian emperor showed no inclination to hurry.

"Forty ships, thirty-five-billion interplanetary credits," he drawled, tucking his hands into the wide sleeves of his plum robe. The emperor's unblinking gaze was almost android like, his eyes lash-less, the irises golden without a dark pupil.

He was quite personable in other ways, having greeted Dale with a wide, welcoming smile upon his arrival two days ago, inviting him to partake of palace hospitality. Xenia was uniquely beautiful, and he had been treated like an honored guest. Any other time, he would have enjoyed himself, but not when so much remained uncertain.

The hunt for Alonio.

The next step of his relationship with Illumina. Would she consider remaining on Deceptio indefinitely?

After two days, Dale began to suspect the emperor's hospitality was a delaying strategy. He'd about lost patience when he'd been summoned to the negotiating table. For a man who ruled a nation of pacifists, the emperor drove a take-no-prisoners bargain.

In truth, Dale could accept the counter of thirty-five-billion credits, but he could drive a hard bargain, too. No sense leaving money on the table. However, negotiations had dragged on long enough. The time had come to move it along and get back to Illumina. "Forty billion," he said, his tone clipped.

The emperor paused for so long, Dale wondered if he'd fallen into a trance. Then the Xenian ruler shook his head. "Thirty-eight—*if* you deliver all forty craft within four years."

With what they were already building, to produce ten ZX7M a year would necessitate a considerable staff increase.

Ping! A code-red message from March shot into Dale's brain. An icy stream traveled down his spine even before he opened the encrypted communique.

You need to return now. Alonio has Illumina.

"No!" He leaped to his feet, knocking over his chair.

The Xenian ruler cocked his head, his expression hardening. "Excuse me?"

How? He paced. What the hell happened?

Charlie let him in.

"Charlie did?" Dale shouted. How was that

possible?

We have him in custody in the brig. But Alonio left Deceptio with Illumina. If we hadn't let him go, he would have slit her throat.

"Charlie?" The emperor frowned.

"I'm sorry." Dale closed and opened his fists. "I have to leave." He got halfway to the door, when the emperor spoke again.

"Is this how Terrans negotiate—"

He looked at the emperor but didn't see him, focusing on piecing some sense into messages streaming into his head. He didn't give a shit-fuck about ships right now. How the hell could this have happened? He hadn't informed Charlie of the threat against Illumina and the requirement for heightened security, but his assistant shouldn't have been manning Flight Control at all.

"There's been an emergency," he explained. "An abduction. I'm afraid I can't continue the negotiation. I have to go."

Sonny was attacked. If he wasn't a cyborg, he'd be dead, but he'll pull through.

Get Carter on a comm line. The Cy-Ops director was supposed to coordinate the security, and instead he'd had his thumb up his ass. Where had Carter been when all this was going down?

He never should have left. Motherfucker! He'd never forgive himself. He should have postponed the delivery, sent someone else. Anything. Charlie was the last person...

"Of course you must go," the emperor said readily. "I assume speed is of the essence. The ZX7M is probably faster than your transport. Why don't you take her, and deliver her when you can, and we'll talk then," he suggested.

"Thank you." Dale leaped at the offer. If he pushed Baby to the max, he could get back to Deceptio in half the time it had taken to get here. His heart pistoned in his chest, human emotion overriding attempts by his nanocytes to lower his anxiety.

Um...Carter's not here. He's been evaced to Cybermed. I don't think he's going to survive. He lost an arm and a leg, his femoral artery was severed, and he damn near bled out. I shot him full of nanocytes, but without a core microprocessor to direct them, I doubt it had any effect. Brock Mann has stepped in as interim director and mobilized Cy-Ops.

"Your excellency, thank you." Dale saluted and ran.

The emperor must have contacted his people at the launch site because he found Baby prepped and ready when he arrived at the pad. Dale boarded and sent a message to his Deceptio pilot to follow on the other craft.

Once out of Xenia's atmosphere, he switched to manual so he could override the cruising presets and push all the power to the ship's engines. Stars blurred as the craft shot through space like a missile. He kept a steely grip on the nav stick and allowed his microprocessor to take over operating the craft. His human brain was too fucked up to concentrate.

This was all his fault. He'd promised to protect her, and he'd failed. His arrogance had delivered her back into Alonio's clutches. Illumina had warned her ex would find her. She had tried to leave Deceptio, but he hadn't let her. He'd forced her to stay by threatening to lock her up. And then he'd sailed off to Xenia.

What the hell was I thinking? Illumina, I'm sorry, baby.

The one mission that couldn't be allowed to fail had—

No. They'd get Alonio, and if he had harmed one hair on her head, Dale would kill him. He'd keep him alive long enough for the Faria to learn firsthand what it was like to be wingless then he'd rip off his other limbs.

Truth? He would kill him anyway for what he'd put her through in the past.

She'd warned her ex was unstoppable. What if she had been right? What if no one *could* protect her? Two cyberoperatives, two of the most powerful, well-trained fighting machines, had been unable to prevent the abduction.

He had to stop the seesawing doubts that could undermine the rescue. In Cy-Ops you completed the mission by focusing on the objective. His mission was simple: save Illumina, kill Alonio. In that order.

Deceptio appeared on the screen, and he keyed in the landing coordinates and turned control over to Baby's computer. Gnashing his teeth, he hailed Flight Control to gain access to the descender. He couldn't get in—but Alonio had. What a pathetic joke his security was.

He'd been undermined from within, once again betrayed by an insider. How could he have been so blindsided? Why had Charlie done it? To his knowledge, his assistant had no beef. Could it have been for money? Had he have traded Illumina's life for a few credits?

Before the dock finished attaching to the craft, he popped Baby's hatch and launched himself out. March bounded up the steps. "I'm so fucking sorry."

Palm up, Dale stopped him. "Focus on the rescue. Talk to me. Tell me what you know." None of this was March's fault or Carter's or Sonny's. It was his. He'd put Illumina in a situation where she was forced to depend on him for protection, and then he'd let her down.

"He had her before Sonny and I could get here. He landed late at night. Charlie had lured her to the dock by telling her you were arriving. It appears she met up with Carter along the way. I think he tried to protect her—the attack was vicious—but somehow he managed to transmit a partial message to Sonny and me. I don't know what the hell that bastard is, but he can transform his right arm into a saber and a dagger."

March handed Dale a bundle of gray, brittle straw wrapped in a cloth.

"What's this?"

"Illumina's hair. Alonio cut it off." March hesitated. "It, um, seemed to cause her considerable pain."

Not pain. Agony. Dale pinched the bridge of his nose. He'd sworn to protect her... He swallowed the lump in his throat. "Faria hair is innervated. Cutting it off would have been like cutting off her fingers."

"Shit."

"Let's get her back before he does anything else." Dale clutched the lifeless bundle of straw. *Her hair. Her fucking hair.* They descended the steps two at a time. "Tell me the rest. Don't sugarcoat it."

"He threatened to slit her throat," March said. "Sonny tried to get a jump on him, but Alonio sensed it and stabbed him, literally in a flash. It's like he can shift matter into energy and back to matter in the blink of an eye."

"How is Sonny?"

"Recovering. His liver and a lung were nicked. Nanocytes sealed the wounds. He'll pull through."

"What do you know about Charlie?"

"Huge gambling debts. He owed a lot of credits to some bad people, and the time had come to pay up. Alonio swooped in and saved his ass. The dipshit thought he was some sort of guardian angel. He knew it was suspicious to request entry to Moonbeam, but since Alonio is an AOP ambassador who'd saved his skin..." March shrugged. "He's scared shitless, now."

"He should be scared shitless. I might kill the little fucker." Right after he crossed Alonio off the list of living beings.

"Brock Mann and Kai Andros are en route. Every available Cy-Ops team member past and present is searching. The AOP has notified its member planets that Alonio has kidnapped Illumina and is to be considered armed and dangerous. Faria has been cooperating also."

Yeah. Now they were. But they had abetted this monster, turning a blind eye to his atrocities. Alonio may have wiped their computer records, but he hadn't erased their memories. Farian authorities had done nothing to protect Illumina.

Not that he'd done any better. He'd tried, but he'd failed, leaving her when she needed him most. Self-loathing bubbled up to burn his throat. He needed to punch something.

Alonio could take her anywhere and then—

I love you, Dale.

Tricks. His mind added voice and emotion to her imagined words. Feelings were easy to guess. No superpower required. No magic involved. But the sensation of sentience, of presence... The only thing he could compare it to was when she'd integrated into his software during orgasm—

Holy shit.

What if—

He stopped dead, his boot landing hard on the shop floor. "*Illumina!*"

"Are you okay..." March stared as if he'd lost it.

Help me, Dale.

Lao-Tzu, Buddha, Jesus. It was her.

He concentrated hard. She could communicate with him, but could he reach her? *Illumina? Speak to me, babe. Where are you?*

Chapter Fourteen

Cold in the unheated cargo bay seeped into Illumina's aching bones as she crouched in the Invisi-cage, unable to stand or stretch without sustaining a severe electrical shock. Back muscles cramped.

The roar of the engines drowned the ringing in her ears.

Alive. But for how long?

Alonio strode in. He'd swapped his bloody clothing for a fresh white tunic and trousers. His hair, braided with a silver thong, fell to midback. Even when committing murder he appeared impeccably groomed. He looked every centimeter the esteemed, urbane diplomat everyone believed him to be. Not at all like a homicidal sociopath until you peered into his silver eyes and noted the absence of mercy.

How had he deceived so many people for so long?

His lips curled into a smirk. "How are the new accommodations working out?"

The Farian language had no word to express her hatred, but the Terrans did. "Fuck you."

Once the craft had launched and cleared Deceptio's atmosphere, Alonio had beaten her nearly unconscious and imprisoned her in the cargo bay, readied with the Invisi-cage. She couldn't access the computer to shut down the electrical field without going through current, which delivered an agonizing shock.

"I'll give you credit," he said. "You were a little more difficult to find this time. You severed most of the psychic conjugal bonds. All but one, in fact. But one was all I needed to locate you. After that, it was easy."

One single filament. How close she'd come to freedom. As soon as she could concentrate, she would break that remaining bond. Not that it would matter at this point.

"Don't you want to know where we're going?" he inquired casually as if he were surprising her with a pleasure flight.

Like she and Dale had done on Baby. Eons ago. Another life. Her heart contracted, and she pressed her tongue to the roof her mouth to stave off tears. She would never see her cyborg again. His friend Carter was dead. Sonny, too, probably. Despair threatened to sap the will to live, but some small spark inside refused to die.

The only good fortune was that Dale had been away when Alonio had arrived, otherwise he would have ended up like the other two men. Dale would have fought to the death to save her. His face formed in her mind. She could picture his laughing eyes, his crooked smile, his hair shorn against his scalp. Dale was tough, strong, powerful.

But not invincible. He couldn't fight a Faria with the transformative gene. The rare genetic anomaly bestowed recipients with great power, but warped their minds. Of the few who had the gene, most were sociopaths. Alonio's nature hadn't manifested itself until after they'd married. And only to her. He'd hidden his condition well. To everyone else, he could appear so normal.

"Aren't you curious?" Her former lifemate cocked his head.

Loathing welled. She hated to play his game, to reward him with the satisfaction of a reply, but ignoring him could provoke another attack. "All right, where are you taking me?" She raised her voice to be heard over the thrum of the engine.

"To Katnia!" He chortled.

She tucked her hands into her armpits to hide

the trembling. "You surprise me. I would have thought you'd prefer to kill me yourself."

A race of cold-blooded bi-pedal predators, the *Ka-Tê* hunted sentients for sport. They'd driven into extinction every non-Ka-Tê animal species on their planet and had to resort to importing prey. The vids she'd seen of them reminded her of the large wild felines on Terra, but hairless and ugly, and far more dangerous. They remained on their own planet, so, unlike Lamis-Odg, they didn't threaten the galaxy as a whole, but the AOP had flagged Katnia as hostile and placed it on its travel warning list. Visit at your own risk.

"Had I thought of it sooner, I wouldn't have removed your wings. The Ka-Tê are partial to beings that fly."

She hated him from the bottom of her heart. "Be careful, Alonio. The Ka-Tê are indiscriminate predators." If she had one wish left, it would be that they tore him apart, too.

Light flashed as his forearm shifted into a saber and then back to flesh and bone. "I'm not worried," his voice boomed, and she realized the engines had gone silent. The floor no longer vibrated.

Her heart hammered, and she ducked her head.

Alonio hadn't noticed yet. *Keep him talking, distracted.* "You won't get away with this. They'll come after you," she said, playing for time.

When he'd knocked her into the nav dash, she'd integrated into the network and installed the code sequence that had caused Baby to stall. But halting the ship only delayed arrival. Eventually, Alonio would notice they were drifting and would investigate. If Moonbeam's computer experts couldn't find and fix the glitch, she doubted Alonio could either, but he might be able to restart the ship, get it to move in fits and starts. They would hobble to Katnia, but they would get there.

"Who? Your friends on Deceptio?" He snorted. "Your *dead* friends on Deceptio?"

Dale wasn't dead. Neither was March. "And the AOP," she said. Until recently, he'd been able to cover up his crimes, but now he'd involved others. The fact that eye witnesses to his atrocities existed and there were records on Deceptio he couldn't erase would change things. But not soon enough. No one knew where they were or where they were headed.

Getting through to him offered the only chance for survival. Hope hung by a thread, a filament thinner than a single hair. Had insanity erased all that he'd been? Or did an intelligent, reasoning mind still exist?

"The AOP is all roar, no bite. Not like the Ka-Tê." A smile lit his face, and he glowed. She still recognized his beauty, but it chilled her that a man so evil, so devoid of morality, could appear so handsome. There should be some outward appearance of his vileness. But it explained why few suspected him, and the ones who did soon succumbed to his persuasion and manipulation. His was the face of refinement unless you peered beneath the surface.

"You loved me once," she said. Had he? She doubted it now.

"I still do, Illumina."

His declaration sickened her, but she forced herself to continue. "Remember our marriage ceremony? We were so happy." He'd been self-assured, doting, and tender as he repeated his vows, and she'd considered herself the luckiest woman alive that he'd been chosen as her mate.

"I remember it fondly. Our wedding was the event of year on Faria. Rulers and VIPs from across the galaxy attended—" He drew his brows together. "Do you hear that?"

If the engines had been running, she couldn't have heard them through the blood rushing in her ears. "I don't hear anything."

"That's right. There's no engine noise." He rushed from the cargo bay.

It wouldn't be long now. Alonio would figure out she was responsible and kill her in a fit of rage, or he would get the ship moving on course for Katnia. She closed her eyes and conjured up Dale, seeing his grin and dancing eyes, hearing the gravelly timbre of his voice, feeling his body against hers, the hardness of muscle, the roughness of hair, the gentleness of his touch.

She cleared her mind of all but memories of him, of the intimacy of their lovemaking and the awareness of his consciousness when she'd integrated into his microprocessor during climax. Her breathing and heart rate slowed.

In her imagination, his presence seemed as real as if he stood in the cargo bay. In her mind, she felt his worry. Love. Rage. Her stomach clenched as his did. Her hands tightened into fists like his. He was determined, ready to march into battle.

How she wished they'd had more time to speak before he'd left. That they'd had that conversation they'd planned for later. Later would never come. For words left unsaid, she wept. *I love you, Dale*. Tears trickled out of her closed eyelids and slid down her battered cheeks. *Help me, Dale.*

Illumina? Speak to me, babe. Where are you?

She jerked. No. His words weren't real. They couldn't be. He was too far away. There was no physical contact to facilitate a mental connection. But if she couldn't be with him, she could pretend she was. *He's taking me to Katnia.*

Fuu— The broken curse sounded just like him. *Where are you now?*

I don't know. He locked in me in an electronic cage in the cargo bay.

Are you hurt?

Illumina squeezed her eyelids tighter, afraid to open them in case the delusion evaporated. *He cut my hair*. Her head and battered face throbbed.

I know, sweetheart. March found your hair on the shop floor.

On the shop floor? Her eyes flew open. This couldn't be hope, imagination. Was she truly communicating with him? *Is it really you?*

It's me babe.

She'd snapped. She'd gone as crazy as her ex. Tell

me something I don't know. Say something I wouldn't think of on my own.

Um...uh...Mares eat oats, and does eat oats, but little lambs eat ivy.

What? What was he saying? It didn't make sense.

It's an old Terran children's nursery rhyme. When spoken, it sounds like gibberish even though it has meaning.

Dale! She burst into tears.

Don't cry, sweetheart. I'm coming to get you.

He'll kill you like he did Carter and Sonny.

No, he won't. I'll be fine. Sonny will be fine.

No mention of Carter. She sucked back the tears. She had to stay strong until he could find her. You know now what he can do. He can harness energy and transform it into matter. His arm can turn into a saber, a knife, or, I suspect, anything he wants.

I can handle him. If Charlie hadn't let him in, he never would have gotten to you. I'll find you—

The door slid open. Alonio clenched his fists. "What did you do to the ship?"

Chapter Fifteen

Illumina? Are you there? She'd been inside his head and then she wasn't. "Illumina!" Dale shouted, anxiety flooding him in a wash. *Don't panic. Anything could have severed the transmission.*

Focus. Focus. He concentrated, trying to bring her back. Nothing. Shit.

March stared at him like he'd lost his mind. "Are you all right?" he asked.

"Illumina was in my head," he said. "We were talking."

"She's a cyborg?"

"No. A gifted computer sensate." *After* he rescued her, they would investigate her abilities. Apparently acts of physical intimacy weren't the only circumstances under which she could integrate into his microprocessor.

Dale opened a circuit to Brock Mann of Cy-Ops. *Alonio is taking her to Katnia. Send a ship to intercept.*

On it. I'll also dispatch teams to trace known routes and will continue working a grid search in case he changes plans.

Good idea.

We'll get her, don't worry.

Brock attempted to reassure him, as he'd tried to soothe Illumina. The awful truth was failure was a possibility. Not for an instant did he doubt justice would prevail. That part they could control. The manhunt would continue until Alonio had met his end. But would Illumina meet hers before they could rescue her?

The idea was too horrible to contemplate. He blocked consideration of possible explanations for why the transmission had cut out.

Focus on the operation. Keep a clear head. For Illumina's sake, her abduction needed to be treated like any other Cy-Ops mission. If emotions interfered, he wouldn't make the best decisions.

Bored with Moonbeam, he had longed for more action, more excitement, to be involved with Cy-Ops again. *You got what you wished for. How's it working for you?*

It sucked.

Dale looked at March. "How long will it take to install a cloaking device on Baby?"

March rubbed his chin. "A couple of hours."

"That's a hundred and nineteen minutes too long." he replied, and signaled a flight line worker.

"Move Baby off the launch pad and prep the Lamis-Odg craft," he told the man.

"Right away, boss." He sprinted off.

"Walk with me," Dale said. "I need to suit up."

"You're going to try the anti-piercing body armor?"

"This is as good a time as any to test the prototype."

"I didn't know it worked against bioelectromagnetic weapons," March said.

"I don't know that it does, but it's the best thing we've got." It was the *only* body shield they had—not that he intended to get close enough to test its effectiveness. Knives and sabers were short-range weapons. If he remained out of reach, he would be okay.

Blaster trumped saber. He'd take several of the former and some microexplosive devices. The MED-21 targeted soft tissue and wouldn't compromise the ship's hull and result in them all being blown to bits or sucked into space. In his plan, only one of them ended up dead.

"There's a lot of area between here and Katnia,"

March said. He'd been in on the comm link with the other cyborgs.

"I know." He raked a hand over his head in frustration. "Intercepting the arrival of the shuttle once it reaches Katnia is no problem. Depending on his current location, that could take a day or two. Who knows what he'll do to Illumina on the way? He cut off her hair! I have to get her away from him as soon as possible."

"She didn't give you a clue where they were?"

"No. She didn't get the chance." Dale expelled a breath, forcing back the worry that edged in. "But I'll find them."

They approached the office stairs. "I'll get the weapons. Do me a favor and grab the body armor from the testing lab."

"On my way." March turned to leave.

"Mr. Homme!" Jesse the Arcanian hurried across the shop floor.

Not now. He bit off an expletive. He'd given the Arcanians a fair shake by hiring them, but dealing with them required an extraordinary amount of patience on the best of days. And today was not that day.

"I'll handle it," March said under his breath.

"Thanks."

Bug-eyed bastard is lucky he's still alive, March communicated via wireless. He got up on the dock and bumped into Alonio as he was leaving.

"I need to speak to you. Mr. Homme!" Jesse skidded to a stop. Dale didn't stand on ceremony. Employees either called him by his first name or "boss," which was more a term of affection than authority, although no one doubted he was in charge. "It's a matter of vital importance." Jesse enunciated clearly instead of mumbling the way he usually did.

Had Jesse's Terran improved?

Didn't matter. Didn't care. "Later, Jesse." He turned toward the stairs. There was no time to spare.

"We'll talk tomorrow, Jesse," March said.

"No. I must speak to Mr. Homme immediately, and my name isn't Jesse—I am agent Wivo of AOP Internal Affairs," he said, and produced a badge. Son of a bitch if he wasn't legit. "We have had Alonio under investigation for crimes against the galaxy."

Dale blinked and glanced at March. Until the abduction, he'd gotten the idea the AOP had all but awarded the Faria a free pass. The AOP meant well, but they focused too much on political correctness to be effective when affairs got nasty. In a galaxy where terrorists like Lamis-Odg attacked innocent bystanders in worship to their mythological Great One, predators like the Ka-Tê hunted sentients for sexual pleasure, and dangerous sociopaths like Alonio were allowed to ascend to power, nasty didn't begin to cover it.

While a dialogue with Wivo might be informative, more exigent matters demanded attention. Talk would not rescue Illumina. "I'll be happy to meet with you at a future time. As you're probably aware, we have a crisis. I'm leaving to bring Illumina back."

Would Alonio go straight to Katnia or detour with the assumption he'd had a tail? The longer the delay in departure, the farther away he would get, lessening the chance of interception. Every second counted. Not finding Illumina was unacceptable.

"That is the matter I wish to discuss." All six of the Arcanian's eyes focused on Dale's face. "It would help, would it not, if you could pinpoint his location?" From his vest pocket, Wivo extracted a small device. "I planted a micro-transmitter device on his person. You can track him with this."

Dale hoisted Wivo up by the shoulders and planted a kiss on his mouth before setting him on his feet.

Wivo wiped his face. "Mr. Homme, that was so inappropriate."

* * * *

The calling of her name brought her to consciousness. The cold, hard metal floor pressed against her throbbing cheek. Sticky. Her face felt sticky. Blood? One arm curled awkwardly beneath her body. Hurting. Why? A whisper of caution had her stifling a groan of pain, and then she remembered.

Alonio's rage. The beating. He'd shut off the cage, yanked her out, and kicked and shoved her to the bridge. Slammed his fist into her face. "Fix it!"

"I don't know what you're talking about!" she'd lied. His punch had smashed into her temple, knocked her to the ground.

By the remaining sprouts of hair, he'd shaken her like a child's toy. An undercut to the abdomen had punched the wind from her lungs. She couldn't breathe, couldn't speak. He rammed her face against the nav dash. Blood spurted from her nose, adding to the red streaks across the computer screen from before.

She had to delay arrival on Katnia. If they got there, she would be gutted before Dale could rescue her. Although, given Alonio's escalating madness, he might kill her himself long before then.

If you kill me, you die, too. Dale's brotherhood of cyborgs would see to it. Telling Alonio that would do no good. His insanity had progressed too far for him to respond to reason or even self-interest. Nothing existed of the man she'd known since childhood, whom she'd married with expectations of a promising future.

"Fix the ship!"

The next blow had hurtled her into blackness, and she knew no more until regaining consciousness on the floor of the bridge.

She lay in silence and pain, her eyes squeezed closed, but her ears and tactile sensations open. She could hear Alonio breathing, but no engine hum or vibration. The ship was still inoperative. He'd failed to get it started. Despite her peril, smug satisfaction flowed through her veins. He wasn't the computer sensate he thought he was. But that had fueled his rage. He'd been unable to undo something she'd done. In that one thing, she'd bested him.

And paid the price for it.

Illumina! For goodness sake, answer me!

Her eyes flew open as Dale's thoughts flowed into her brain.

"You're awake, good!" White boots appeared in front of her face. Alonio hauled her to her feet. Bile belched into her throat on a booster of agony, and malevolent features faded to gray.

She staggered and fought not to retch. *I'm here.*

So am I. I'm in a cloaked spaceship right behind you.

Her eyes widened. It was fortunate her face was averted. She schooled her features to blankness.

Are you all right?

I'm okay. Not as good as before, she answered truthfully. *But okay.* Still alive. That's what counted.

Is there a chance you could open the emergency launch bay? In the event the ship became inoperable, spacecraft were equipped with escape pods programmed to land on the nearest inhabitable planet.

I think so, but there's probably a pod in the bay. You'll have to eject it.

Light flashed, and a blade stroked her throat. "If you do not repair the ship, I'll kill you now." Her skin stung as he nicked her. A rivulet of warmth trickled down her neck and between her breasts.

Illumina nodded. "I'll try," she lied.

"You'll do more than try."

He flexed his wings then folded them into place. His shove sent her sprawling into the pilot's chair. She slid a hand onto the bloodied screen.

I have to focus on the computer, she signaled. She couldn't communicate with his microprocessor and the ship at the same time. *I love you.* She choked.

Don't say that like it's good-bye. Pause. I love you, too.

If Dale succeeded in sneaking aboard—and it was a huge if—he would still have to contend with Alonio, and he had no idea the monster her ex had become. If he missed the narrow window of opportunity to board, and she restarted the ship, his little pod would not be able to keep up.

"What are you waiting for?" Alonio snapped.

"I'm trying to find the error."

"Hurry up."

Computer, open emergency bay shuttle launch door.

"Switch to voice command so I know what you're doing." Forearm shifted into dagger.

"Computer, activate voice mode," she said aloud, while thinking, "*Computer, countermand previous order and launch escape pod.*

A faint rumble shuddered through the craft. Fear doubled her heart rate.

Alonio cocked his head. "What's that noise? That's not the engines. And why isn't the computer speaking?" He shoved her hand off the screen and palmed it. "Computer! Voice mode! Report!"

"Escape pod launched," the computer said.

He backhanded her. Her head slammed into the padded seat. "What did you do?"

"I'm sorry! I made a mistake! I couldn't concentrate with you standing over me."

"Computer, close the emergency bay," he barked.

The bay couldn't have been open more than twenty seconds, scarcely enough time to eject the pod. Dale couldn't have gotten onboard.

Alonio pressed his blade to the underside of her jaw and drew blood. "I don't know what you think you're doing, but if you don't have this ship started in ten seconds, I'll slit your throat."

She could have pointed out that without her, he would drift in space until he died of starvation because he no longer had an escape pod, but attempts to reason with him would lead to an abrupt end to her life. Out of options, she palmed the screen. Streams of code flashed through her mind. She inserted herself into the line of marching numbers and changed the single digit that hung everything up.

"Prepare for re-propulsion," the computer said. "Re-igniting engines." With a jerk, the craft surged forward.

Sheathing the dagger, Alonio dragged her out of the chair then hauled her down the corridor to the cargo hold. He sandwiched her between the door and his body and planted his palm against the entry module. She choked, fighting to remain positive.

Maybe Dale would get his pod back on his ship and would catch up with them again. Perhaps there would be another chance for a rescue. Hope wobbled under despair wrought by the facts. She would not get another opportunity to open the bay to let him in. He could follow the ship, but he wouldn't be able to board. If only she'd had a few more seconds on the bridge...they'd come so close. *Oh, Dale. Dale!*

I'm right behind you, sweetheart.

Illumina gasped.

Alonio whipped around.

Her cyborg stood in the corridor.

Cara Bristol

Chapter Sixteen

Alonio dragged Illumina in front of him as a starburst of light shot out of his wrist. A dagger unsheathed, and he pressed the blade to her throat.

Way to go, Homme. He'd fucked up already by calling out to Illumina, allowing Alonio to react. Focus on the objective. Don't let emotion get in the way. Personal feelings impede outcome.

"One step closer, and she dies," Alonio said.

Marshaling his willpower, Dale suppressed his rage and forced himself to ignore her bloody and battered face, her chin-length, jagged hair, and focused on his target. "If she dies, you die," he said with deadly calm.

In pieces. In Cy-Ops, he had taken out many an enemy, but he'd never tortured anyone to death. The Faria would be the first.

Dale held his blaster level, his microprocessor calculating the odds that he could pull the trigger faster than the Faria could sever an artery. He had an edge of .4 seconds, but if Alonio's body fell, the knife could cut her anyway. Too risky.

Until something changed, they were in a standoff.

"Drop your weapon," the Faria ordered. "Or I'll kill her now." No idle threat. His gaze radiated crazed determination; he was willing to commit suicide to murder Illumina.

Dale didn't fear for his own life, but he would do anything to keep Illumina alive and well. Besides, he had other weapons. He slid his finger off the trigger and across the barrel. Maintaining eye contact, he bent and placed the weapon on the floor.

"Kick it away."

He gave it a gentle shove with his foot.

Illumina's gaze shifted downward. *If he moves, I can try—*

No, Illumina.

He blocked her thoughts to avoid distraction. He didn't dare make the same mistake by allowing emotion to cloud his reason. Keep the focus. The mission would be victorious, his might would overpower the enemy, and she would survive.

"Release her, and I'll allow you to live," Dale said.

A couple of seconds of opportunity or a couple of centimeters of space between the knife and her throat was all he needed.

"Do you think I'm a fool?"

"It isn't just me you have to worry about," he said. "You're a wanted man. Half the galaxy is searching for you. The AOP won't let this pass this time."

"Bureaucrats don't worry me. You don't worry me. Remove your utility belt."

That could be a problem.

Alonio twisted her hair around his fist. "I don't have to kill her all at once." With his knife arm, he sawed through the hair next to the scalp. She screamed.

Dale unclipped the weapons belt to which he'd holstered two other blasters and three MED-21 charges.

"Toss it over it here." Alonio motioned with the knife.

His two-second, two-centimeter break.

Dale grabbed a blaster before the belt hit the floor. He went for the head shot, but the Faria's knife arm transformed into a shield, scattering the photon stream in a spray of sparks. With a cry, Illumina wrenched away. Her ex latched onto her dress. She struck at his face with her fist, landing a blow near his eye.

A raucous Farian cry of rage rocked the craft.

Dale shot off another blast. The shield came up in time to block it. Sparks sizzled.

He fired again.

Alonio released her, and she dove for the blaster, but her ex kicked it out of her reach. Hiding behind the shield, he scooted backward then disappeared down a side passage.

Dale scooped up Illumina. "Are you all right?"

She nodded.

He picked up the blaster and pressed it into her hand. "Go to the bridge. Lock yourself in. You can do that, right?" With her computer ability, she could change the codes, block entry.

"Y-yes."

He snapped on his belt and grabbed another weapon. "I'm going after him. Contact March. Tell him where we are. He'll contact Cyber Operations." He brushed a gentle kiss to her swollen mouth. "Don't open the bridge until I come back—or Cy-Ops gets here. Understand?" He didn't think Alonio could best him, but the transformation from dagger to shield had been an unpleasant, unexpected development. Dale didn't like surprises. His weapons

226

outpowered any knife or saber, but if the Faria created a blaster-type weapon…

"Be careful," she said.

No promise on that one. He would do whatever it required to solve the problem. The Faria would be brought to justice—cyborg justice. Swift and permanent. "Go now," he said.

Illumina hesitated as if to argue, but then she nodded and headed down the passage. Dale sprinted after his quarry.

What would the Faria do now? Would he hole up? Mount an attack? Or attempt to flee the ship? Alonio could be lying in wait, plotting an ambush. *Make no assumptions. Check and verify.*

A passage that may have been a maintenance channel because it was almost too narrow for Dale to squeeze his bulky cyborg body through broke off from the wider aisle. He flattened himself against the wall and peeked into the passage. A fireball zoomed by his ear. He jerked to avoid having his scalp singed. The wall lit up red-hot upon impact.

Good news: he'd located Alonio.

Bad news: he did have other capabilities.

Keeping as much of his bulk shielded by the wall as he could, he peered into the passage. Within a millisecond, his cybervision detected the target, his body hidden behind his arm-shield except for his wings, rising over his shoulders like two swords. Dale squeezed off a shot. It skimmed over the shield and hit the tip of his left wing. The Faria bellowed with pain. The satisfying stench of burning feathers wafted through the corridor.

How do you like it, asshole? This is for Illumina. He fired again, hitting lower on the wing. Alonio roared and his armor disintegrated, but before Dale could react, another fireball whizzed down the corridor, forcing him to take cover behind the wall. Maybe, before he killed the asshole, he'd pluck him alive.

Dale stole another glance. The shield was up again. Switching between flamethrower and shield and absorbing a blaster hit had to be draining. Perhaps if he kept the Faria shifting, his energy would be depleted. He fired off three blasts in quick succession. Two hit the shield; the third burned through an already-singed wing. Alonio roared. The top quarter of his right wing had been reduced to its skeletal frame.

Before his enemy could shoot off a retaliatory fireball, Dale stepped into the open and blasted down the passage, alternating between shield and wings. If Alonio's energy ran down, he might lose his ability to transmutate altogether.

The asshole must have realized it, too, because he retreated at a fast clip. Crap. The passage fed into the starboard corridor where the escape pod bay was located and where Dale's craft was docked.

A much smaller man than Dale, the Faria scooted through the narrow corridor with ease. Dale had to suck in his breath then inch sideways while firing to prevent Alonio from getting off another fireball and toasting him like a roast in the oven. But no way would he allow him to escape and continue his reign of terror against Illumina.

Alonio reached the end of the passage. His shield shimmered.

Oh. Shit.

You okay? March's communique zipped into his brain.

Armor transformed to flamethrower. *Oh, shit.* Dale fired. The fireball blew right through the photon steam and slammed into Dale's chest. Heat flashed upward, and the shock wave threw him backward several meters. Reflex averted his face, squeezed his eyelids shut.

When he dared to peek, his shirt was melted onto his prototype body armor, but other than a first degree burn on his face, which his nanocytes rushed to heal, he was fine. The Faria, however, was gone.

Peachy, Dale replied to March. Good news. I've tested the body armor, and it works.

A Cy-Ops team is on its way. ETA in twelve minutes.

Roger that. Hope they've got a fire extinguisher.
What?

Nothing. Homme, out. By the time Cy-Ops arrived, Alonio would be a name in history.

No longer in danger of being crisped he hastened though the passage and entered the starboard aisle. Vacant. The Faria hadn't wasted time making himself scarce.

Plastering himself to the wall to minimize target size, he raced for the emergency bay to cut off the escape route.

The Faria's reign of terror ended today. Right here. Illumina was armed and protected on the bridge; a team of cyborgs headed their way. Perhaps he should wait until backup arrived, but this was personal. *Fuck with Illumina, you deal with me.*

His opponent might stick around to fight some

more, but the smarter move would be to leave the ship, lay low until he recovered his strength, and then mount a new assault. Except Alonio didn't think rationally—he'd already proven his willingness to sacrifice his life if it meant Illumina would die.

Dale would sacrifice his life if it meant she would live.

What would the unpredictable Faria do? Would he fight or flee?

A guess and a gamble. If he went straight to the pod assuming the asshole had chosen to flee, but the Faria had opted to fight, Alonio might double back and go after Illumina. If he acted on the assumption Alonio would fight and he turned the ship inside out looking for him, but the Faria had fled, he would get away, and they'd be forced to deal with him later.

Search the ship or head off the escape? Emergency bay, he decided. If Illumina had done as Dale had told her, she should be safe.

Stay on the bridge, he transmitted to Illumina.

Silence.

Illumina! Blood pressured spiked. Why wasn't she answering? Dale didn't think her ex could break into the cockpit. He hadn't thought he could get on Deceptio, either. What if Alonio had gotten to the bridge? What if the door melted under a fireball? Or what if Alonio created an electronic zapper to fry the computer circuits?

Illumina! Are you all right?

No answer. Forget the emergency bay, forget searching the ship. He pivoted to check on her.

She marched toward him. "I'm here," she said.

Why did women never do what you told them to? "You were supposed to stay on the bridge." How could he keep her safe if she was running around the ship?

"Alonio's getting away. I saw him on the monitor," she said. "He's in the emergency bay. He's trying to break into your escape pod. I tried to contact you, but I couldn't get through. By the time I heard you calling, I was already here."

His fault. He'd blocked her so he could focus, wouldn't be distracted by her distress. "It's still not safe. Go back to the bridge," he ordered, and ran for the emergency bay.

Through the door's viewing window, he spied Alonio, singed wings drooping, entering codes into the spacepod's keypad.

"Oh, no you don't. You're not getting off the ship and you're not taking my pod either." Dale's fingers flew over the computer screen, trying every code his microprocessor could come up with, but the system was frozen.

Emergency bay access had been stymied by a computer sensate. But Alonio faced a challenge, too. Did he recognize the Lamis-Odg origin of the escape module and realize the password was written in the Odgidian language? Battle of the hackers. Whoever gained entry first would win.

Illumina touched his elbow. Damnable woman. She didn't listen very well. "Let me," she said. She nudged him aside, palmed the screen, and closed her eyes. A moment later, she sucked in breath. "Clever."

That didn't sound good. "What is?"

"He's inserted a mutation code to alter the password when you apply the PIN."

"When did he do that?"

"About three minutes ago. Basically, he's locked down the system."

"Can you free it?" Dale didn't take his eyes off Alonio.

"I'm working on it."

It killed him to stand and wait, but her hacking skills exceeded his. She was their best chance to open the emergency bay. *Hurry, Illumina, hurry.*

He couldn't hear through the reinforced walls, but there was no misunderstanding the triumphant fist pump. A second later, the pod hatch sprang open.

"He did it." The bastard would escape.

The Faria straightened, turned around, and made eye contract. Smirking, he saluted then stepped toward the open hatch.

This is only the battle, not the war. But failure burned in Dale's gut.

Illumina pressed her lips together. "It's not over yet. I'll bet he forgot one set of passwords." She palmed the screen; her forehead furrowed in concentration. "Computer!" She inhaled. "Open emergency bay shuttle launch door."

Alonio's eyes bulged and his mouth yawned in a silent scream as the ship's external wall slid open. The escape pod, tethered by a lock-down, remained in place, but the vacuum of space sucked Alonio into the blackness. His body inflated like a giant winged balloon as blood gasses bubbled underneath his skin. He flailed arms, legs, and wings in a desperate, futile attempt to fight his way back to the ship. Though Illumina couldn't see the effects of the extreme cold, with his cybervision, Dale could. Mouth, eyes, and nose—the watery parts of his body—froze over.

Within moments, his skin turned blue, and frantic movements slowed. In 13.2 seconds, struggle ceased altogether. His heart no longer able to pump, Alonio went limp as he passed out from the lack of oxygen.

He drifted away to meet death. Dale opened a line to Cy-Ops, cancelled the extraction, and requested recovery of the body.

Illumina closed and re-pressurized the bay. Her lips quivered. She burst into sobs.

Dale enfolded her in his arms and rocked.

Killing someone was never easy. Not even when the bastard deserved it.

Chapter Seventeen

Two weeks later

Dale folded his hands behind his head as Illumina disrobed. Health, well-being, and luminosity had returned since her abduction a fortnight ago. Even the night terrors had abated. The artificial light of Deceptio's underground habitat bounced off spiky, silvery hair already growing out.

Her smile was pure seduction. "Like what you see?"

"You know I do." His erection tented the thin spread tucked beneath his armpits. She approached the bed, and he tossed back the covers so she could join him.

She eased onto the mattress and faced him. Arms and legs entwined in a comfortable tangle. Her thigh slid between his legs; his arm found its place beneath her head.

Despite Alonio's demise and her physical recovery, the score had yet to be evened. Dale did not consider the matter finished. There could be no forgiveness for the Faria's crimes. He was dead, but

237

Illumina had not received justice, and he ached to give it to her. He often replayed the final scene, wished he had been the one to open the hatch and shoot Alonio's body into space. Wished he'd been able to drag the still-alive, bloated Faria back in, rip off his wings, and eject him again. Death had come too quickly. Illumina's cuts and bruises had healed, her hair was regenerating, but the loss of her wings remained permanent and painful. Unless...

"You're thinking about him, aren't you?" she asked.

"Are you reading my mind again?" He had to be careful.

"No. It's written all over your face." She touched between his brows. "You get an intense look when you think of him."

"Sorry." He kissed her. He focused on how her sweet breath mingled with his, her face so smooth against his cheek, the bold way she kissed.

"That's better," she murmured and squeezed his erection. Soft fingers fondled with a firm touch the way he liked. Her thumb swiped over the head.

He groaned in submission to her caresses, his body strung between relaxation and tension. With every stroke, every caress, his desire ratcheted higher and higher, organic cells and robotic nanocytes vibrating with need and demand, buzzing in harmony. His emotional human and his analytical cyborg were never more integrated than when he was with her. She loved him as he was. Understood him. Accepted him. She'd given him a soft place to fall, a place he hadn't known he'd been searching for. With her at his side, in his bed, he found completeness.

His one wish was to give to her what she had given him.

He'd gotten the go-ahead this morning. The one time he'd broached the subject of cybermed pain management, she'd refused to discuss it. So he had to keep his secret until he could *show* her in hopes that seeing would convince her. Since the rescue, their mental bond had strengthened. Telepathy occurred with ease, and, during intimate encounters, almost automatically. So he'd locked his plan behind a firewall and hoped it held.

He never wanted her to think he required more of her than what she was. He loved her scars and all, but he ached for her loss, her pain. She could be prickly, sensitive, so he had to show her before he could tell her. Even then she might reject the idea.

The proposal didn't come with guarantees, only a

gamble, and he had no wish to reopen painful, old wounds. Brock had sent him updates on Carter's recovery, and the idea, first rejected as impossible, then as too risky, had grown into something possible. Maybe...

He wrestled with doubt on an hourly basis. What if it failed?

Holy fuck, what if it succeeded?

She's going to find out, if you don't stop thinking about it.

Putting his thoughts on hold was easy enough to do when she closed her fingers around his shaft, lighting a hot fuse that traveled into his abdomen and set him on fire. A sure grip, a firm squeeze, a long slide, and *Lao-Tzu, Buddha, Jesus.* He stopped her before he tumbled over the brink. He cupped her breasts and thumbed nipples already hardened for his touch, massaged her clit, and combed his fingers gently through her hair, even more sensitive during regeneration.

Her soft moans excited him as her touch had done.

Illumina signaled her readiness by grabbing his shoulders to pull him on top. He resisted, trying to maneuver her onto him. Good-naturedly they wrestled.

"We've done it this way before," she argued.

Once. But *her* pain caused him discomfort. "It's not good for your back." Nor did he care to risk injuring the remnants of her wings at this critical juncture.

"My back may never improve beyond what it is. Are we never going to have sex that way?"

"Never is a long time." He won the tussle and pulled her on top of him.

She tsked. "Next time..." She lowered herself onto his cock and began to rock.

He groaned. "I'll look forward to it." He palmed her breasts and thrust his pelvis, meeting her stroke for stroke. Pleasure shot through his body in an undulating wave, driving him to the edge again. She neared her own climax, her head flung back, her face contorted in a rapturous grimace, ripples in her pussy tightening around his dick. Shuddering, they climbed the heights of ecstasy.

Next time we do it my way. He heard her voice in his head.

She was persistent. Her stubbornness didn't surprise him. Tenacity had kept her alive when she had nothing else to protect her. Maybe next time indeed. He'd been smart to erect the firewall.

While passion subsided to a warm throb, he held her, caressing her back, her skin slickened by perspiration.

"Are you packed and ready to go?" he asked.

She nodded, her head bumping his chin. "We'll be gone a couple of days or so?"

"Or so." At least a month. He'd debated how much to tell her; after all, she had the highest stake, but he felt in his gut it would take more than words to persuade her.

"I'm so thankful Sonny and Carter survived. I'd never be able to forgive myself if they'd died because of me."

"It wasn't your fault. I called them in, and everyone in Cy-Ops accepts the risks, *especially* Carter."

"He couldn't have known about Charlie."

"No. If anyone should have, I should have." He'd been a cyberoperative for goodness sake. If he'd investigated more thoroughly, he probably would have learned about the gambling addiction and recognized the security risk from the start. People with vices or vulnerabilities were easily exploited.

By that reasoning, he never should have hired

Illumina. She'd been the biggest risk of all.

Not hiring her would have been the biggest mistake of his life.

"Desperate people do desperate things," she said.

"Yes." In truth, there'd been no malicious intent to Charlie's betrayal, only a desire to repay a perceived debt. He believed his assistant when he claimed not to have known what Alonio, an AOP ambassador, had intended. Still, Charlie should have known *better*.

While his assistant had broken no planetary laws, only Moonbeam procedure, his actions had nearly killed three people, two of them with Cyber Operations. Cy-Ops would neither forgive nor forget.

"How long do you think Cy-Ops will keep Charlie?" Illumina asked. Under the circumstances, past and future, she had a need-to-know about the clandestine organization, so he'd come clean. She'd guessed everything except the name of the outfit, anyway. His Faria was smart.

"Carter will decide when he's back at the helm."

"I'm so glad I have the chance to thank him for everything he tried to do for me. How much longer will he be at Cybermed?"

"Probably another month. The surgery to replace

his lost limbs and to implant the microprocessor is the quickest part. Working out the synchronicity between his human brain and the processor takes a bit." It wasn't like rolling an android off the assembly line.

He sought her gaze. "Cyborgs are still human," he said. "Or Faria, or Lamis-Odg, or whatever race they were before the computer and mechanical mods."

She scowled as if he'd implied she was cyberphobe. "I know that."

That's what he counted on.

Chapter Eighteen

Three weeks later

Late in the evening, the workout/training area of the Cybermed facility was deserted except for one man on the running machine.

"He's bigger than he used to be," Illumina murmured as they watched Carter push his biomimetic legs to the limit. Although he'd lost only one leg to the saber, Carter had opted to replace both with cyber prosthetics to maximize function and strength. The Cy-Ops director had been a tall man, but now, like his cyborg brothers, under the influence of nanocytes, he'd added bulk. Deltoids and pecs bulged; abs rippled.

"Faster, too." Dale clocked him at ninety-six kilometers per hour, the equivalent speed of a cheetah, the fastest Terran land mammal.

"I can hear you," Carter called with only a slight pant.

"His hearing's improved, too," he whispered. She giggled.

"Computer, decelerate and halt running

machine," Carter ordered.

When the deck rolled to a final stop, he leaped off, snagged a towel then strode toward them. "Taking off tomorrow?" He wiped his face.

"At the break of dawn."

"Back in a couple of months, right?"

"That's a fair estimate. After I finalize the contract with Xenia, recruit and train a shop overseer and a replacement for March, we'll report to Cy-Ops for active duty." It hadn't taken much arm-twisting on Carter's part to get Dale—and March, too—to re-up.

No job could replace the pulse-throbbing, heart-racing missions, but he hadn't re-enlisted for the adrenalin rush. All across the galaxy, people met life-threatening situations like Illumina's. Somebody had to fight for them. He could be that somebody—as long as he didn't have a personal stake in the outcome. He never again wanted to confront a situation where the life of someone he loved was in jeopardy. "When are you heading back to HQ?" Dale asked.

"Day after tomorrow." Carter chuckled. "If I don't show up, Brock will dispatch a team to drag me in. He says if he has to spend one more day behind the console he'll go batshit crazy.

"While you're recruiting for your replacement on Deceptio, I'll be searching for an assistant to manage the day-to-day stuff so I can get out in the field." He twisted his mouth. "I'll be the most knowledgeable but inexperienced rookie field agent Cy-Ops has ever had."

"You'll handle it. Your Intel background gives you a huge advantage. That's more than any of us had when we started," Dale said. "All you have to do is adapt to new and improved parts, which it appears like you're doing." He jerked his head at the running machine. "You looked good out there."

"It's amazing, really. I don't feel that different as a cyborg. Maybe fitter and healthier and more rested." He flexed his biomimetic arm. Synthetic arteries and veins delivered blood to and from regenerated skin and muscle, supported and strengthened by a titanium humerus, ulna, radius, carpus, metacarpus, and phalanges. "It still surprises me when I lift something that only a power-model droid can lift."

"I know the feeling," Illumina said, and stretched her composite wings to their full extension. With a slight motion she lifted up into the air and hovered then lowered herself to the ground. Her face glowed with happiness, framed by waist-skimming silvery hair. Under the influence of nanocytes, her hair had grown to its full length in record time. "I never thought I'd be able to fly again." As if they'd always been a part of her, she fluttered her wings then folded them close to her body. The transition had been a breeze for her.

Harrowing for Dale, wondering throughout the process if it would work. There'd been so many hurdles to overcome. Could Cybermed docs design prosthetic wings like they did arms and legs? Did he dare raise Illumina's hopes that she might fly again? And was she willing to become a cyborg to do it? If the wings were built and attached, would they work?

The answer to all four concerns turned out to be yes. Cybermedical engineers had fabricated the first ever biomimetic wings. They'd removed the leftover nubs that caused her so much pain then strengthened her spine before attaching super-strong but ultralight wings created from a composite material skeletal structure and thousands of small vanes resembling silvery feathers.

Her wings were not indistinguishable from real biological parts the way prosthetic arms and legs were, yet they suited her.

"I'll never be able to repay you for what you've given me." Her eyes glistened with tears as she glanced from Dale to Carter.

"You don't owe me anything," Carter said. But his signature and resources had made it happen.

Dale had feared she would reject the idea, so he'd brought her to the Cybermed installation to watch the process, to see Carter's improvement and that of other men and women whose conversion to cybernetic organism had given them not just a new lease on life, but a reason to live. After Illumina had jumped on board, he'd worried that the cyberengineering docs wouldn't be able to do it. They had leapt at the challenge and had transformed impossible into done-deal. Science had created a miracle.

Illumina had become the first cyborg Faria. She didn't have the same kind of microprocessor the rest of them did—hell, as a computer sensate, she could out-program, out-hack any cyborg alive, but her computer chip allowed her brain to control her flight. Nanocytes enhanced her body's ability to heal itself and granted her immunity to most known diseases.

If Carter could race against a cheetah, Illumina

could probably outfly a peregrine falcon—and whip up a small tornado at the same time.

Carter had yet to see more than a liftoff. "Show him, babe." Dale nudged her.

With the merest murmur of sound, she rose off the ground and hovered overhead, her radiant smile as wide as her wingspan. With a graceful flap, she climbed nearly to the roof before swooping in a dive and then soaring around the perimeter of the high-walled workout gym. Beauty in motion, she glided with the grace of angel. Laughter rang like chimes singing in the breeze of her wings. His heart swelled. He could watch her all day.

"Wow," Carter said. "She's something, isn't she?"

"Yes, she is." She had been *something* before she'd gotten wings again. It was her elation, her unfettered happiness that he loved to see.

She'd been offered an appointment to AOP ambassador, replacing Alonio, whose death had been reported as a tragic accident, but she'd turned it down when Carter invited her to work for Cyber Operations.

In truth, Carter probably wanted Illumina onboard even more than Dale or March. Brains counted more than brawn any day. Such a perfect spy she would be. The enemy would be too distracted by her beauty to realize she'd hacked into their computers and stolen their secrets. She might be the edge Cy-Ops needed to take down Lamis-Odg. She could literally fly circles round the best hacker alive, but no way would Dale allow her to venture into the field alone. She needed some muscle as backup. So they were partners. And lovers. That was the best part.

The air caressed his face as she landed beside them. Silver eyes sparkled. Her hair snapped and crackled.

"Cyberengineering outdid themselves," Carter commented.

"Agreed," Dale said.

She folded her wings and slipped her arm through the crook of his and hugged him. Soft breasts pillowed his arm. Heat rushed to his groin.

How soft she would be under him...yes, "next time" had come. Now they could do it in the "traditional" Terran way without risk of injury or pain. They also did it standing up while she fluttered her wings. And with her on top. Cowboy style, doggie style. Side by side. They were still exploring their many and varied options.

I don't know why my flying turns you on. Amusement glinted in her eyes as she'd caught the drift of his thoughts.

Everything you do turns me on. His mouth twitched.

She blushed like a Faria. She turned silver.

Carter glanced between the two of them. "Oh geez. Get a room."

"Good idea." Dale winked at her.

Race you to it! Illumina lifted off and flew for the door.

"Catch you later," he said to Carter and ran after her.

~ The end ~

Watch for Cy-Ops Sci-fi Romance 4, to be released early summer 2016. To be notified of all new releases, subscribe to my author newsletter. http://eepurl.com/9aRJj

Books by Cara Bristol

Cy-Ops Sci-fi Romance series
Stranded with the Cyborg (Book 1)
Mated with the Cyborg (Book 2)
Captured by the Cyborg (Book 3)

Breeder series (Sci-fi romance)
Breeder (Book 1)
Terran (Book 2)
Warrior (Book 3)

Rod and Cane Society (spanking romance/bdsm
light)
Unexpected Consequences
False Pretenses
Body Politics
Disciplinary Measures
Reasonable Doubts
Irresistible Attractions

Other Titles
Goddess's Curse (Fantasy romance)

Captured by the Cyborg

Long Shot (Corbin's Bend Spanking Romance)
Longing (Paranormal)
Stolen Moments (Romantic Comedy)
Naughty Words for Nice Writers
(Nonfiction/thesaurus)

About the Author

USA Today bestselling author Cara Bristol has published more than twenty-five erotic romance titles, including contemporary and science fiction romance. No matter what the subgenre, one thing remains constant: her emphasis on character-driven seriously hot erotic stories with sizzling chemistry between the hero and heroine. Cara has lived many places in the United States, but currently resides in Missouri with her husband. She has two grown stepkids. When she's not writing, she enjoys reading and traveling. To learn more about the author, visit her website at http://www.carabristol.com, friend her on Facebook at http://www.facebook.com/carabristol3, or sign up for her author newsletter, http://eepurl.com/9aRJj.

Acknowledgements

I owe a huge, huge debt of gratitude to editor Kate Richards and copy editor Nanette Sipe who went above and beyond the call of duty in fast-tracking this manuscript. Jaycee of Sweet 'N Spicy outdid herself on this cover. I'd also like to thank Lisa Medley, my street team, and all my readers and fans.

Made in the USA
San Bernardino, CA
08 March 2016